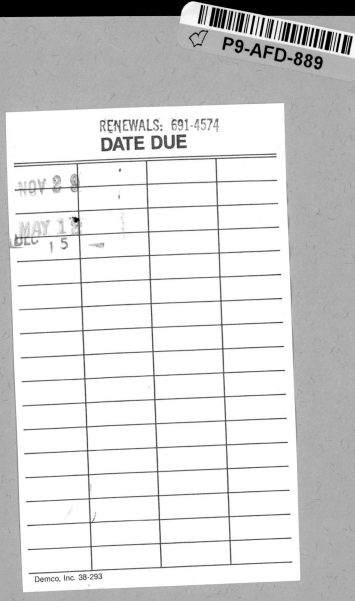

BACK BEFORE
THE WORLD
TURNED NASTY

BACK BEFORE
THE WORLD
TURNED NASTY

―――――――――――

A Collection of Short Stories

―――――――――――

Pauline Mortensen

THE UNIVERSITY OF ARKANSAS PRESS

Fayetteville   London   1989

Designer: Chiquita Babb
Typeface: Linotron 202 Bembo, with Perpetua
Typesetter: G & S Typesetters, Inc.
Printer: Jaco Bryant Printers, Inc.

The paper used in this publication meets the minimum requirements
of the American National Standard for Permanence of Paper
for Printed Library Materials Z39.48-1984 ⊚

These stories have appeared in the following magazines: "The Window Effect" and "Rat Reunion Summer," *BYU Studies;* "The
Course of the River," *South Dakota Review;* "Side Effects" and
"Modern Rustic " first appeared in the *Cimarron Review* and are re-
printed here with the permission of the Board of Regents for Okla-
homa State University, holders of the copyright; "Woman Talking to
a Cow," *Phoebe;* "Conditions in General" and "House Painting
Deal," *Hayden's Ferry Review.*

Back Before the World Turned Nasty was 1988 recipient of the Utah
Arts Council Publication Prize. Its publication is supported by the
Utah Arts Council.

Library of Congress Cataloging-in-Publication Data
Mortensen, Pauline, 1950–
Back before the world turned nasty : a collection of short stories /
by Pauline Mortensen.
p.   cm.
ISBN 1-55728-104-1 (alk. paper). — ISBN 1-55728-105-X
(pbk. : alk. paper)
I. Title.
PS3563.O88164B33   1989
813'.54—dc19   89-4739
                                                          CIP

For Elouise Bell——back before.

CONTENTS

———————

BACK BEFORE
THE WORLD
TURNED NASTY

THE WINDOW EFFECT

My arm is being fed from a bottle. I am awake and very much aware of how much my life is not my own. It is part of the room, part of the bed, part of the bottle, part of the nurses when they come in and check that part of me that is theirs. I cannot move, so they move me. Every few hours they come in, four of them, and turn my body—that part that is theirs. There is a plastic tube that drains the excess blood out of my back, drawn through the tube by the sucking action of the expanding canister that sometimes gets tangled underneath when they turn me, gets tangled and sometimes lies next to my face, and I can see that part of me that is no longer a part. And there is a wire holding me together in my back, holding me together, keeping me separate from the room. But it doesn't work; I am part of the room.

There is an old man in the next room. There are many old people on this floor, the orthopedic floor. He is in a box-like sling, so I am told, because he has a broken hip. But there is much the old man does not understand. He struggles against the straps that restrain his body, struggles and shouts obscenities in German, and in English he calls, "Gut me out off hair, somebody!" He speaks for both of us.

Facing the window, I see that it doesn't open. Windows should open. A person may have to crawl out of one in an emergency someday—to save himself. I've been thinking of crawling out of a window lately, that part of me that is still mine, that isn't attached to wire and tubes and bottles and canisters. I call it the window effect.

I first became aware of the window effect when I was teaching a Sunday school class of five-year-olds. The manual said they were five-year-olds; I didn't doubt the manual. I found out later they were six and seven. I think there might have been a lack of relevance. Eldon was seven. One day while I was talking about "Our Heavenly Father Made Our Bodies," Eldon climbed out the window in the back of the room, slipped over the sill to the ground before I could get to the part about "our two strong legs take us to church." I suppose he needed the fresh air; I certainly did. Looking back on it now, I can see the advantage of building churches all on one level, close to the ground with windows that open, not like hospitals that leave you windowless and groundless on the twelfth floor.

The nurse comes in to take my temperature. Her wrist snaps as she shakes the mercury down. "How are we doing today?" It is a cliché, I know, but they really do say it. It is their way of letting you know that your body is not really yours but theirs, to measure, to rub, to pump up, to turn over, to wash, to patch, and to puncture. The last time the technician took my blood, he said it was a nice color. He added the tube that was a part of me to a collection of tubes he had on his tray and went on down the hall.

The man next door. "You gut no rights ta keep me. You lemme go."

The nurse puts the thermometer in my mouth, wraps my arm, and pumps it up to take my blood pressure. They have to monitor the vital functions. I am alive. She brings the bedpan.

Last week the old lady across the hall attacked the wire-haired nurse. She went for the nurse's throat. The nurse was trying to put the oxygen tubes back in the old lady's nose. Personally, I think if she had the energy to attack a nurse, she probably didn't need the oxygen tubes in her nose in the first place. Then later when I called for a nurse, that same nurse with the black wiry hair came in and shut the door, didn't ask what I wanted, just came over and sat down. (I wanted my toothbrush.) She gave me the story of her life. Said she didn't know if it was worth it. I assumed she meant nursing, so I asked her why she became one in the first place. She said it wasn't like she thought it was going to be. I didn't have any answers. Staying in the hospital wasn't what I thought it was going to be either. She brought me my toothbrush. I counted three cases of the window effect that day: me, the nurse, and the old lady across the hall. I have a nephew who had an especially bad case.

When Steve was two, he'd sit on my lap and name off the makes of cars in my Matchbox car collection. I'd give him hugs for every one he got right, and he'd careen through the list again. It seemed as if he were building up an early immunity. But at sixteen he came down with it like the rest of us. Don't ask me how I know these things. I just know. He slept in the basement, and instead of using the door like a civilized person, he started climbing out of the basement windows. He mashed down the flowers all around the house. It wasn't as if anyone were going to stop him from going where he wanted to go. He just wanted to avoid any questions.

Steve owned a Yamaha, and you know what they say about them, the part about someday you'll own one? I guess if he can do it, anyone can—climb out a window and ride away from it all on a motorcycle. Of course, some people have tried to explain Steve's behavior as a means of escaping his father, but somebody will always say that. Personally, I think Steve rather enjoyed those father-and-son outings to the traffic court. At one point, they wanted to send Steve away to an institution of some kind. I didn't think clinical caring was the answer then, and I haven't changed my opinion.

The nurse takes the bedpan. Talcum powder on the rim helps.

Sometimes when the doctor listens with his stethoscope, the metal disk is cold on my chest; and sometimes he forgets to put the ear pieces into his ears. But he says I'm fine just the same. That's the way they do things here.

In the recovery room, they shook my arm to wake me. I didn't know how long they had been shaking it; it seems as if there is more shaking in there than recovering. The boy next to me was recovering from his wart-removal surgery. They shook his arm for a long time before he came to. Then he tried to climb off the bed. I was hoping he'd make it, but three of them held him down.

Anesthesia is a trick anyway. They tell you that you won't feel a thing. But when they shake you back to an awareness of life, there is pain that wasn't there before, is there for no apparent reason, and won't go away by closing your eyes. It's kind of a medical jet lag; you come back out of time, out of sync with what you remembered last. It is no way to treat a patient, even if he does survive.

Steve owned a Yamaha, but my window is puttied in. The doctor comes through the door. It's Saturday, and he is wearing a yellow sweater and brown pants.

"How are we doing today?"

Part of us looks like we are going to play golf while the rest of us stays here.

"Pain," I say. "Those pills make me sick; you got something else?"

"I'll change you over from Percodan to Tylenol-3. That should take care of it. Anything else?"

"No," I say. What can I say? He's done his part, performed the operation.

The doctor operates on Tuesday. Before surgery, he listens to rock music on his portable radio to get his adrenaline up, or so the rumor goes. So on Tuesday, his bedside manner is different. I have five pillows on my bed, and last time he asked me if they were proliferating. Today he says, "Anything else?"

"No," I say. What could he give me on his three-minute visit? He has done his part and deserves his diversion. But I'm not altogether sure which is the bigger diversion, the golf or the surgery.

The doctor finishes writing on my chart. He says, "See you Monday," and goes out into the hall. My free arm pushes the button that shuts the door behind the doctor, pushes the button that raises my head. Stop. I close my eyes.

When I was six my sister, Eileen, made me ride a horse against my will. She wanted me to be brave. The horse bucked me off, and I was knocked into semiconsciousness. She carried me into the house, screaming melodramatically the whole while, "Speak to me! Speak to me!" I remember, but she doesn't. It's fun to bring up at family reunions to tease her with. My legs hurt for weeks. Like they do now; like they've done for years. Perhaps a faulty memory is not altogether a bad thing; it's a liberation of a sort, not escape necessarily. I don't blame her for anything. Why should she blame herself? In family, I think it can be a healthy thing, forgetting.

The pain pills help forgetting. As a great joke I brought a book by Faulkner to read called *As I Lay Dying*. With me slipping in and out of forgetting, the book makes even less sense here than it did at home. But I want to forget, to go back to the trickery of anesthesia. Always there is something that reminds me of where I am. The bed is hard. The bottle is dripping into my arm. I must circle today what they will feed me tomorrow.

7

Sounds like a life of leisure, I know; I can't help that. In the afternoon when I press the UP button all the way until it stops, I can see the park across the street, the children on the jungle gym, children urging "higher" on the swings and "faster" on the merry-go-round. There are trees in the park that shade people eating lunches underneath. I have air conditioning.

My husband comes to visit me every night after work. He says this is harder on him than it is on me; he can't sleep nights. I let him bring me things—it helps him, makes him feel useful. He sits in the chair by the side of my bed and falls asleep watching television. He sleeps fine here. Then he goes home.

It's the same thing when I'm home, but I'm not complaining. People keep telling me that children make a difference. I don't doubt it. But so far I haven't noticed that it's solved anything.

I've been making a list of things I would like to do when I recover from surgery in a year or two; having a baby is not on that list. There are things I've not been able to list for awhile: tennis, racquetball, fishing, cycling; dishes, pies, beds, carpets. I'm not making a joke. Maybe being able to do something for a change will make a difference.

It's eight o'clock. The nurse brings in my breakfast and takes away the lid from my plate.

In Rathdrum, Idaho, near where my mother lives, there is a cult of devil worshipers who make their living waylaying cars on the prairie roads. They smash in the windows of the cars that stop at desolate intersections, knock the windows and the people out with gunny sacks weighted with rocks. Sometimes they link arms and make a human chain across the road to make the cars stop.

It's not a weighted gunny sack I want exactly; no one needs that much attention. But the human chain is not such a bad idea. Of course, there's always a chance that the cars will not stop. A friend of my mother's says she was driving home alone one night across the Rathdrum prairie. She just barely made out the human chain while there was still time to build up her speed. It didn't make the papers because the devil worshipers take care of their own, and the lady wouldn't have reported it. But someone found an arm lying in the field next to the road. I don't know that it was worth losing an arm over, but something must be.

Of course, there are other types of human chains, like the ones in movies where they stretch themselves across a flooded river, wrist to wrist, fingers digging in flesh, in order to get everyone across safely, to escape the rushing flood.

I butter my toast and put on the jam that comes in the indented plastic form.

My roommates at college accused me of using my back as an excuse to get out of doing my share of the cleaning. It does sound suspicious; I can't help that. I don't need to justify myself anymore; the doctor has my x-rays for anyone who cares to look. But I don't think anyone will bother. I sure wouldn't, even knowing what I know—that a human chain might stop the speeding enigma; that is, at least it has been known to stop it in movies and on deserted highways. That may be so, but it certainly doesn't sound like a very safe thing to do. Perhaps something more subtle would work.

I eat my whole-wheat toast and prunes and watch out the window at the swaying treetops in the empty park, the branches writhing like Medusan snakes above where the children usually play. The great stone face of the hospital faces the park, and I am a part of the hospital.

CONDITIONS
IN GENERAL

My mother and I are crouched in this log together, sitting in charcoal and red mud with a wall of wood and roots around us. The hailstones drone against the outer bark. We are on my brother's planting job in the Nez Percé National Forest in central Idaho, where forest winds have uprooted isolated trees left over from the logging operations—the harvest. We are here planting seedlings for the money: my mother who is sixty-five, in her hooded green sweat shirt, making enough to pay for a furnace; and me, making money for tuition, and thinking about my husband still in Utah at his regular job. I am here against his wishes, but after being married ten years, I can get away with that. Then, too, it helps if you don't have children—it's easier to be "liberated." So I am here inside this rubber raincoat, sweating in the cold.

It was barely light this morning, the distant tree line a mere shadow picture knuckled against a white wall when we tied our lunches and our raincoats around us and began the two-hour hike to the planting job. Perhaps what made me start thinking about conditions was falling into the creek as we crossed over on a slippery log. Being wet, muddy, and miserable is nothing new here for any of us, but it is not appreciated, especially at six in the morning on the way to work. The thing is, no one thinks to bring extra clothes for emergencies, and besides, there isn't enough room in the Suburban. So with my brother and his crew already halfway up the mountain, the Suburban locked behind us on the road, and camp hours away, my mother and I stood there knowing that one of us was going to be very uncomfortable for several hours until the sun came out. But then knowing that the sun will come out eventually and dry everything stiff by noon is no great comfort to someone who has just fallen in an icy creek. So it is the obvious time to start thinking about conditions, conditions in particular, conditions in general. This is usually what I try to avoid.

My condition—the state of being unpregnant. I used to write letters to anxious relatives about my "condition." It used to be a great joke.

I slip the tips of my fingers between the charcoaled log and the small of my back, pushing with my fingers so the knuckles can massage the tender spot above my hips. My mother looks at me. She understands the advanced stage of my condition, this topic that is delicate for us both.

This morning after crossing the creek—and me falling in— we crossed the snowdrift and loaded up our trees from the tree cache where the Forest Service has buried them in the snow. We packed the trees into our planting bags, and after climbing the hill to the first road, my legs chafing from the cold and wet, my mind balked, and we sat down on a log by the bank. Perhaps with movement and circulation things might have been different. But there we were on a logging road that could have been passable by four-wheel drive, so that we didn't have to walk. You see, the Forest Service does not like tourists in here, in the charred depths of their forest. People write nasty letters to the editor when they see the slashed and burned areas, and the barren tree plantations where contractors have dozer-piled the log debris and where the Forest Service has fired away the brush, leaving charred logs, burned-red topsoil, and white ash. This is called "soil preparation," and it scrapes away the topsoil into sterilized heaps, disturbing the ecological balance, causing the ground squirrels to multiply at infectious rates so that they gnaw away the tree roots when you plant the trees. Under these conditions, it is unlikely that the forest will be restored. But everyone makes a great attempt anyway.

To keep out the tourists then, the Forest Service plows up the roads in six-foot mounds twenty-five humps to the mile, strung out like knots on an umbilical cord—plows them up to keep out the tourists and hunters, though they say it is to save the road from the spring runoff. These are the conditions.

And I was angry at that, and at other conditions, sitting there thinking that in spite of everything, when the reports are turned in and they indicate a low survival ratio for the trees, it will be recorded as tree planter error. It will be my brother, the contractor, who gets the blame. But I will feel the anger, too—out of a sense of family pride—because culpability is a frustrating matter, something that isn't assessed until all contracts are expired and chances for recriminations dissolved. Then it only affects your reputation.

Everyone hopes that this job will be different, that the Forest Service here will stop trying to lay the blame on the planters, and stop treating us as if we are here to rip off the government. The specifications say that we must dig a twelve-inch hole. But when the topsoil has been scraped nearly down to bedrock, it is impossible to dig a twelve-inch hole, and they spend all their time digging up our trees to ensure that we have dug a twelve-inch hole. And this is in spite of the fact that the specifications also require that we use the regulation mattock that has only an eight-inch blade, instead of the twelve-inch mattock made by my brother. There is one exception. In lieu of digging a twelve-inch hole, you may select a tree with shorter roots. But the roots are the only thing that are twelve inches around here. And it is next to treason to trim these roots or plant them in an "s" or "j" shape in the hole. They watch you for this, but say nothing at all about conditions, about the rocks, and the topsoil that has been scraped away, or the ground squirrels. These conditions do not exist in the manual.

My mother is still optimistic about this job, but I am overwhelmed. Hiking in this morning, I was struck by the fact that we can protect the roots, keep them wet, guard them from the air into the hole, but there is only so much that we can do. It is recorded as tree planter error when the trees die, and each year the Forest Service comes down harder with regulations that make no sense at all when they give you trees that have broken dormancy or have molded before you get them, and are, therefore, already dead. So they watch us closer each year. It is the contractor's reputation in general that is harmed. My brother can say nothing, or he will end up losing his contract, possibly his bond, and may have to pay the government for lost time and dead trees.

There is always the possibility of getting into another kind of business, but we are all optimistic fools about such things.

This morning I was overwhelmed by these conditions. And a thirty-year-old girl sitting on a log with a bag of trees strapped around her waist, crying, is not a pretty sight I would imagine; I was a force to be reckoned with. So when it started clouding up, I think that that may have had something to do with why my mother suggested we crawl into this burned-out log instead of staying out in the hailstorm.

I'd like to stretch out the cramp in my leg, but there is no space. My back is curved with the arch of the inside of the log. If conditions had been different, I would not be in here. Perhaps I would be home in Utah seven hundred miles away; at the least I would be in the Suburban five miles down the hill on the main logging road. But the storm caught us by surprise. So here we are.

I have never seen my mother run from a storm before. I have seen her plant through the snow, fighting frozen ground to get the trees in, until my brother came and told her they were quitting for the day because it was too cold for the trees. The roots froze in the air before you could get them in the ground. (The cold kills the trees, but only leaves your fingers numb inside your gloves.) Until my brother comes, she always works on. This is why I was surprised when she looked up at the darkening sky and said we'd better find shelter.

I think working indoors has always been a luxury to my mother, who has always hauled hay, thrashed wheat, and fed cows. Working inside doesn't require bundling up in men's clothes and straining against the weight of buckets or bales. She insists that she was one of the original women's libbers, the ones who protested *against* working outside with the men. Now at sixty-five her protests are retired, and she pulls her hooded green sweat shirt closer around and tucks her hands under her arms.

Perhaps she would never admit to wanting to stay in the house and do "women's work." What she says is that she expects to recline in heaven beneath the shade of the trees she has planted. On hot days out on a bare hill it's an accommodating thought—when the sun is frying your brains, money doesn't count for much. But she survives, and football players from the employment office only last three days up here before they quit.

So in spite of the fact that we usually work through the weather, here we are inside this log. This is why I suspect that she did this for me, is still protecting me, even though I am married and living away from home, and she is in her sixties. I am confined here, but protected.

I never did get used to wearing men's boots, like my mother sitting cross-legged next to me, her neoprene soles caked with red mud, her wool socks rolled down over the top to protect her laces. I wear old Adidas that ooze out the warm water when I push against the charcoal, old shoes that suck it back in—cold. The men's boots pinch your toes, leave them numb for months. In the tent, I rub my mother's feet, warm them next to the catalytic heater. I squeeze the bones of her metatarsal arch, and she says it feels so good—when I stop. Underneath, she has been walking on a ball of deformed bone that she didn't know should not be there. I grab her big toe and try to shake it back into feeling, but she'd rather I left well enough alone. I smooth cream over the calluses, and she pulls on her anklets for the night.

At night we play cards and talk about the Forest Service, and this keeps my mind off conditions.

When I was seven, our Guernsey cow became ill. I found her in the corral, groaning and rocking back and forth, a slick, brown calf-back protruding through a large stretched circle beneath her tail. When my mother came, she wouldn't let me see any more. She made me stand back behind the railing, and I had to go up the cattle chute and get glimpses through the bars. The veterinarian couldn't come right away, so she called my brother Bernell, who came over because he was the oldest and had done these outdoor things before. He said it was a breech birth, and from behind the chute I watched him put his hand on the calf and push it back into the mother, then saw him put his arm in up to his shoulder to turn the calf around.

From the first I had wanted to see because it was such a horrible and intriguing thing, and because I wanted the calf to be mine. I had visions of raising it myself, naming it, and feeding it, teaching it to drink the formula milk by letting it suck my fingers as I lowered my hand and its head into a bucket. I wanted to be there when it first bleated out into the world, and when it stumbled to its feet. It was something you might see on *My Friend Flicka,* and it all seemed like a reasonable expectation.

But the calf was born dead. And seeing the mangled-limp nothing lying in the ditch my brother dug, the dirt being shoveled in and bouncing on the bloated belly, there seemed to be an inconsistency in the promise—a promise that all women secretly believe in perhaps.

It starts with mud pies served on cardboard plates, served out to rubber, lifeless mannequins. Such things start the idea of the promise, the storing and recording for future use that is all intended to the one end.

At college, the first time through, I studied children's literature, children's reading, and children's psychology. I got a degree to teach children, but that was not the purpose. Most people who take those courses do not intend to teach strangers. So my files are obsolete: files of children's books, files of poetry, files of pictures mounted and laminated for sticky fingers.

There has been a progression in this, cutting out patchwork squares for baby quilts, piecing them together with sly smiles at my husband as he watched TV, smiles that dissipated as one by one I gave away my stockpile of knotted quilts. In those first years there were imaginary cravings that would send Denny to the store laughing to please me, but this, too, has become a joke that we punch each other with.

And what are the final stages of this condition? There are operations for this—operations a woman must go through to save herself. It is the doctor's desire to restore you to the "function" for which you were intended, but they do not say this. They say, "We will fix you up. How long has this condition persisted? I will arrange for a time with the hospital." And after that, "Come back on the twenty-fourth."

So I come back and back, but eventually discover that the promise itself is conditional, based on patience and longsuffering, temperature, timing, and time, longevity and hormones, procrastination, endurance, and chance. The chance is not so great as it once was.

16

The doctor says, "This is a minor operation which involves a scraping of the uterus." And then at another time, "Cauterization sometimes increases fertility." But both forms that I have to sign say these methods are not always effective and may result in a worsening of the condition, pain, infection, cancer. But this is the exceptional condition. I sign anyway.

I sit here bent against my own insides and wait for the rain. Mother swings her legs out of the end of the log and begins pressing the hailstones into the mud with the tip of her boot.

I am the last of ten children, the spoiled one. The first one was born with a stomach defect, one they didn't know how to cure at the time. They gave it medicine and goat's milk, but it died. Mother had nine more that lived, nine who grew up to be obnoxious adults for the most part. And now in her sixties, she is through with having children.

The pelting eases. The rain makes red streams that begin to course through the white ash, forming irregular trails round the exposed roots of the log. The sun filters through the rain, and my ears seem to pulse with their own hollow sound in the absence of hail.

They say that the color of the ash is an indication of the temperature of the fire. The hotter it gets, the more the soil is irreversibly burned into a white acid powder. When you plant, you are supposed to avoid these hot spots because nothing will grow there. I can believe this. When it rains, the water collects on the surface in black and red slime, but underneath it is dry white ash. At times it seems like my mind has burned into dry white ash.

Some people, like my mother, still see God in nature, in a beautiful sunset, a quiet pond, a blade of grass. I get sick of that. My mother, who has raised nine children, fully expects in the next life to raise the one that died. After fifty years, she still puts flowers on the grave in anticipation of the resurrection.

But this is nature too, the great Mother Nature, this landscape that has been logged of life, mangled by dozers so that roots and trunks lie piled and partially burned together. Where is God in all of this? Can these people find God in a piece of charcoal? Do we have to bring him into the discussion?

I remember a novel that does this. In *Losing Battles,* set in the middle of the depression, in the middle of poverty, Eudora Welty has Jack Renfro sing "Bringing in the Sheaves" as he treads home with wife and family. Symbolically, he is a soft-bodied chimney swift who nestles down in the bosom of his family, hundreds of them together in the sooted walls of their chimney. Now that is optimism. But pure optimism will never be avant-garde again, so they say. Eudora Welty thinks God is alive and well and living in a chimney. I think God sits on the tree line at sunset and stirs our optimistic imaginations.

Mother begins to sing now, now that there is space for hearing. "Said the thousand-legged worm, / as he gave a little squirm." How many times have I heard that? She used to rock me to sleep with that worm. "Hasn't anybody seen a leg of mine?" Her voice is dry and cracked. "If it hasn't been found, / I'll just have to hop around, / on the other nine hundred ninety-nine."

The rain begins to stop. We sing another one. "Detour. There's a muddy road ahead." This was always our traveling song, passed around just before the cookies. "Detour. Paid no mind to what she said. Detour." We'll never make Ted Mack's Original Amateur Hour. "Should have read that detour sign."

She guesses it's time we went back to work. We crawl out head first into the warm, light drizzle. We straighten ourselves after our confined condition. I take off my rubber raincoat and massage my lower back. The clouds are breaking up and moving away with perceptible speed; the earth is mottled with shade. But even in this shaded drizzle, the sun begins to warm my back, and already there is steam rising from wet logs.

On the fire trail above us is my brother and the bedraggled crew. They have come after us. Compared to them, we are relatively dry. Mother yells something about not having enough sense to come in out of the rain, but they are not laughing. We are all going home before *they* catch pneumonia. Mother and I pretend we are ready to go back to work, but secretly we are glad to quit for the day.

On the horizon, the standing trees flash tentatively with light as wreathing clouds dismember. The men trail off down the muddied slope, and Mother and I follow, winding around logs and roots like optimistic centipedes. Our boots slide in the ashen mud, but we keep our balance, and slosh down to the pickup on our feet.

THE COURSE
OF THE RIVER

My father stored his dynamite here in this barn. It sat in its wooden boxes, waiting and threatening, for years after he died—except when my brothers Judd and Harlo took a stick or two out to toss around and explode on odd occasions when you least expected it. After years of this Russian roulette, our mother had Judd and Harlo get rid of the dynamite. I can imagine how they got rid of it. I can see them throwing a stick at a time down some canyon, a stick at a time, after urging the old fuses to burn, first slow then fast, until the leaking, seamy stuff had been "gotten rid of." I suppose that it all went off, no matter what they did with it, and there is not a half box of un-exploded dynamite strewn down a bank waiting to surprise someone in the hot, distant future. But the dynamite is not here anymore in the hay-littered barn where rats gnawed away for generations. I am here in carpeted comfort, in the eaves of the barn at Rock Falls, unbuttoning my pajamas in the heat of the night and pressing my feet against the cold rafters above the loft.

I am here as an initiate—my first snow cat ride into the ranch in the dead of winter. I am the initiate and the dunce. Can I help it if the snow cat keeps getting stuck? Judd complains he is not here to work, not here to pull me out of the powder when in my confusion I let up on the gas to avoid a mere abyss—and land in the powder—or when I gun the snowmobile and jump the abyss and land—in the powder. The damn thing is not supposed to sink in down to the windshield. But it does, and I get yelled at, and we come back to the barn to cool off and warm up.

So my father stored his dynamite here in this barn—dynamite he used to change the course of the river. He blasted away a mile of rock to dig a new channel closer to the mountain, so that the river would run smooth and straight there, and leave the family alone where they were trying to plant a garden and raise chickens in the middle of the meadow. It was a precarious situation then, as it is now, trying to share with a wandering river the narrow space between two mountain ridges. At best it is only a matter of time, until the snow of one good winter floods into the quiet stream and the surging river straightens itself through where we are here.

So we sit here in the barn, which is now Judd's cabin, and play pinochle with Carol Rose, his wife, and Eileen, our sister. Between Judd's complaints about having to wait on three helpless women, we shuffle the cards and talk about old times.

Someone says, "Wouldn't the old man have loved this?" referring to our father, and how easy it is to get up here now, with the spring-cushioned, ignition-start snowmobiles sitting on the porch. And someone adds, "Yes, this is the life. He was just born thirty years too soon."

On the wall above Judd's head are our father's snowshoes, crisscrossed above the window like sabers, the curling, cracked leather now varnished hard. These were the snowshoes he used when he wintered up here, that he used to check his beaver traps up Jordan Creek and used when he made emergency trips to Coeur d'Alene, where he walked full-bearded to see his family, down the paved road out to Dalton.

This was my father before I was born. And I had always heard it said that rather than thirty years too soon, he was born a hundred years too late.

I pull my feet off the cold rafters and slide them back under the blankets. This is my thermostat. The rest of me cooks in the compounding heat that rises to the loft, rises and burdens the breathing air that sometimes condenses on the rafters and rains in my face. This is the thing about Judd's barn. All the heat rises to the top, and Judd sleeps downstairs stoking the fire in a draft.

But I'm not complaining. I could be over at the house where Eileen and I tried to "rough it" last night. Chop our own wood, dig our own snow, that sort of thing. She did not tell me that the stove was temperamental, that if you opened the door for more than five seconds to do something superfluous like stick in another log, the idiot thing would belch smoke out at you; it would stop drawing up the chimney the normal way and start pouring it out through the forty or fifty rust holes around the sides and fill the old homestead house full of smoke inside of ten minutes. She did not tell me this. I was just supposed to know. So as we lay there in bed in our knitted ski masks and our snowmobile suits, the doors and windows wide open so we could breathe, I tried to remember what it was I had come up here for.

After all, I could be home going through the dumpsters behind McDonald's, looking for packing boxes. I should be doing that because after the sheriff's auction next month, my husband and I will have to move. They will be selling our house, not because we lost our jobs and couldn't make the payments, but because the escrow man decided to take our down payment and borrow on our equity and invest it in a gold mine in Nevada.

So we are in transit, after having thought that we were settled. We thought this because we spent almost a year changing the landscape. As a sure sign of our intention to stay, we began scraping madly down to bedrock. We began with the fruit trees. I'd always had the misconception that the Orem bench was a soft alluvial hump, the sediment of a million-year inland sea. I was wrong. It is an alluvial rock pile dumped forcibly from the mouth of Provo Canyon and then cemented together by the clay sediment of a million-year inland sea. We chipped and dug for three days to plant those fruit trees. It was a warning we didn't heed. For the rest of the summer, as we watched our limp semi-dwarf fruit trees struggling for survival in their individually carved saucers of water, we worked on the rest of the yard. We heaped up rock and pushed it aside for the vegetable garden, we wedged it up and pressed it flat for the lawn, and we groomed and cornered it into rocky but incredibly neat flower beds. We did all this in the summer, and in the fall the escrow man, who had embezzled our future, scraped together a few thousand dollars of someone else's money and left town for places unknown.

This has been our experience with buying a house. Our lawyer has since shown us where we went wrong. He shows us in retrospect. My brother says, "You have a college education. You should have known better." But I majored in literary theory. How am I supposed to know about real estate investments? All we wanted was a place to settle, one place to pile all our junk so we wouldn't have to move it for the next thousand years.

I roll to the side to let my back cool. I didn't come here to prove anything, to show Eileen and Judd that I'm still tough, still a Sanderson, and that I haven't become some educated fool who doesn't know how to make it in the real world. I didn't come here for that. I came here to see the snow, to see the house in winter, to see the river and what it's done to my father's place. I came here because I am in transit.

There is something about this place that is instantly invigorating and depressing. It draws us all frantically on like a burn-ing fuse that hisses and fizzles under our stomping feet. It may be the river. Behind the house the frozen river flows idly under the ice. It is not the Mississippi. It is a mere trickle and a river only by definition. There is no hint of the raging torrent that it becomes every spring, the omnivorous beast that has already gnawed its way through a chicken coop, a bunkhouse, a half mile of board fence, a garbage dump, and a clothesline. Last year it took a bite from under the corner of the woodshed not twenty yards from the house. It is a geologic inevitability, the meandering stream in process, leveling our valley and our ranch to a lower peneplain.

We have tried with dozers and backhoes to pile rock, with shovels and axes to erect toothpicks against the spring thaw. What we need is something like the Army Corps of Engineers. By ourselves we have only been rearranging rock.

Our father bought this place during the war, after a long line of spurious enterprises. Before this he tried farming without seed and equipment, dude ranching without horses, and wool raising without sheep. He was going to make his fortune in Karakul sheep, selling the precious black Karakul wool to make coats, until he discovered that it took hundreds of sheep more than his fifteen, and that he had to kill the young lambs just after they were born to take their curly black hides.

Before the ranch, the family was always moving, always packing quilts and dishes and kitchen chairs to a new start. They moved from Rexburg to Bayview, to Rexburg, to Rose Lake, to Linfore, to Pritchard, to Dalton. But he bought the ranch and made a living logging and farming in the woods, after always looking for a way to make money that would not tax his weak heart. It was one long rush to make his fortune before the dynamite in his chest exploded.

I remove my feet from the covers and try the rafters again. The cold moves down my legs, and I throw back my arms for air.

I had not been born yet, through all of these false starts; I've only heard about them around the card table on trips like this one. Even most of what I know of this place is largely second-hand. Sometimes when we come up here, we sit around on the beds that line the living room of the house and bring out all the "blackmail" we can think of. Some of us are better at this than others. I can still remember the time my sister made me ride Old Coalie against my will. I told her it wasn't a good idea with all those other horses running up and down along the outside of that fence. But she made me do it. And when he bucked me off and I passed out, she carried me into the house screaming, "Speak to me, speak to me." I don't know why she doesn't remember this like I do. I remember very distinctly her crying over my limp, battered body. The fact that I was unconscious at one point has nothing to do with it. She says if I was knocked out, how could I remember what happened? She says that I am lying through my teeth in order to make her feel guilty about the bad back I've had ever since. But that's got nothing to do with it. I like to tell the story because she's forgotten it and gets so mad when I tell it and because it is just one of those things that happened here.

So we sit around telling such stories, stories about our father and his exploits with the fish and game department, about the poached deer he would always have in the cellar, about the time he spent in the Kellogg jail for poaching deer, and about the tame fawn that came bounding in the front door and skidded across the linoleum between Dad and the game warden, and the game warden jumping up and saying, "Damn, what was that?" and our father slapping his thigh and saying, "Oh hell, they do that all the time."

I was not even a conscious being when these things happened, but I can tell them as well as anyone. There are stories of other places, of Linfore, Bayview, Rose Lake. But there is a difference between these and those we tell about the ranch, about Rock Falls. Here there is affection, good times. It is the pull of gravity, the settling place, the inside curve of the river.

So we sit around and tell game warden stories, tell about the people who used to inhabit that world of a generation ago. And when we run out of stories about the past, stories about the dead, we disparage living relatives.

Most of us recognize the pull of gravity. We have our family reunion here every summer, and Eileen and I take the new generation up the face of Deer Hill across from the house, so that we can pull weeds out of the rocks before we paint the great letter "S" that stands for Sanderson. Most of us come to the reunion, but there are some who refuse because of hard feelings, because the great bulk of the ranch, which we loved and hated while we were growing up here, was left to Mother when Daddy died and during the sixties she sold it to our brother Galen, and he in turn sold it back to the government from whence it came, all but these ten acres. We all have been crying in our beards about it since. But some fail to recognize our common loss and dally in tributaries, refusing to come back to the main stream.

Basically there are two contending factions in the family, two ways of explaining what has happened. Some of the family explain it this way: "You can't live in the past. You have to support your present family. One way to do this is to invest in real estate. This is a very profitable way. But in order to invest your money, you must divest yourself of emotional attachment. You sit on the property a few years, and then you take advantage of the inflationary trend and you unload." There are several who think this way. They are our rich relatives.

Our poor relatives argue thus: "The ranch is my heritage. It is my ancestral home. Someone has sold my ancestral home for a mess of pottage. The ten acres given back to the family is to appease a guilty conscience. I will not be party to appeasement."

These are our left and our right. The rest of us take the middle ground and make snow cat trips in here so we can sit around and talk about everybody who doesn't think like us.

Then, too, we speculate. Where will my husband and I want to build our cabin? Which acre of the ten do we want? What about one big lodge that all nine of the brothers and sisters could build together? Some will never be able to afford their own cabin. And if they do, what will happen if all nine families and their children's families decide to build their own private shack up here, digging backhouses wherever they please, polluting everybody else's water supply. It could happen. So I am here in transit speculating on my one solid, snow-covered acre.

It goes on and on. We build phantom A-frames and log lean-tos, while the very snow we are sitting on could melt suddenly with one good chinook and wash it all away. We are all poised on the powder of the inevitable. It's all only a great "what if," someone building a retaining wall here, someone tearing it down there, the river surging and wiping clean the scrapings of a former, industrious generation, the river merely taking a wider swing and making an oxbow of where I live. Is that what I came here to find out, to rest my feet on a cold log and be cooked and smoked to death when I could be home packing my kitchen chairs?

Perhaps. But this is the view of the river through binoculars. I am standing on the ground, ground I thought was solid. Where do I go from here? I see my own ignorance, my own misguided judgment in real estate, and my husband's. Let's not leave him out of this. I see this and feel the sand dissolving beneath my feet. So I ask: Where do I insert the dynamite to change the course of the river, or how high of a retaining wall must I build? But these are rhetorical questions. I see more than this. I see the layered rock of ancient peneplains. Yet I see my own incredible need for place in the midst of all this change. I am neither a mover nor a shaker of massive fortunes. I am a settler. And although the face of the land must change, I am still a river-running initiate who has the gall to demand room to drop out of suspension, a shoal, a settling place, a sandbar, on the long inside curve of the river.

MODERN RUSTIC

We carry guns here. It's the new wild west. Protection against the hippies and the Hell's Angels, the new deer hunters and the neo-Nazis. This is their territory, the Idaho panhandle, rural refuge for society's opportunists, nature freaks, and reformers. The land where the deer and the antisocial play. And we came here to build our cabin, our mountain retreat, came because this is the homeplace, ancestral ground, and because the land belongs to the family and we are entitled to our section.

We came here to build our cabin, but it is still unfinished. And Denton and I are lying here on the floor of the old house at Rock Falls doing our exercises, putting all this together. He says if the Hell's Angels come down our road he's ready. All he has to do is slip the bullets into his borrowed .45 and we're safe. I believe it, because he's from Florida and I don't think he knows where the real safety is on a borrowed .45.

So we came here to build our cabin, knowing what we do about the hippies and the Hell's Angels, and knowing that the ranch house where we've been staying has been broken into and picked clean, shot up and knifed, cornflaked and kindled. These are the stories. My brother Judd comes up one year and chases off four guys trying to carry the cookstove out the back door. My sister Eileen comes up some lost weekend and surprises three dopeheads in the living room. Judd's wife, Carol Rose, comes up and finds all the windows shot out. Everybody comes up here and finds all the windows shot out. That's a given. Then there was the summer of the draft, five guys heading for Viet Nam spend their last days of freedom hacking up our beds. Or the summer of the bizarre, thirteen dissected squirrels stretched out gutless in cornflake circles on the kitchen floor. And who could forget the winter of the insane, some guy dodging bad checks, checking out our house at Rock Falls, torching our furniture for firewood, taping up our three best quilts in the house to look like women—a brunette, a paisley, and a patchwork—and finally tattooing our walls with flecks of red enamel floor paint, a strange impressionism like he'd shot his own brains out. These stories have ricocheted back and forth in our heads for the entire summer. We knew all this, but still we came because the land was free.

Of course, all this happened many moons ago. Way back in the seventies. Ya, it's been a good seven or eight years since anyone's taken a crowbar to the kitchen sink. It's a new dispensation, an era of peace.

But there is at least one sincere element of consolation—nobody has ever challenged our presence outright. Vandalism has always occurred in our absence, behind our backs. No one has ever bulldozed their way down the bank from the road and said, "We're taking over. Get the hell out." We like to think about that. And with my brother's barn out in the field, which he turned into a weekend cabin, and my sister coming up just as often to the house, we decided it was safe, safe enough to

show my country relations how a person with a college education can still swing a hammer.

At any rate, we have been here off and on all summer, breaking the mountain stillness with our gas-powered generator and
feeding our drying wet socks to the pack rats. But we are here
now on the verge of going home, poised on the end of a stick,
fabricating how far we have come—the foundation, the floor,
the walls, the roof—but not spending our last heroic night in
the shell of our cabin. We did not come this far to freeze to
death on the last night for a principle. But we have come further than we expected. Further than anyone could have predicted from where we began, with the sun-dried ectoderm of
the old woodshed that had to be stripped down to its internal
log frame. No one could have predicted that the log structure,
held together at the joints by twelve-inch spikes, but shaky as
hell, could have withstood the trip across the field in the first
place. And that after we released the chains from behind the
road grader, we would be able to square it up and come this far.
No one could have predicted it because they didn't think we
had it in us. But here we are, after doing what we could with a
block and tackle, old lumber, and used roofing. As we go over
this, it is like reporting one conquest after the other—the floor
joists nailed along parallel lines, right-angle walls shimmed and
nailed to round vertical poles, and jack pine logs for the loft
"borrowed" from the Forest Service. This last one is a good
one, and Denton rolls over to do his leg lifts.

It has been a summer of adventure, the coyotes howling out
in the dark, trying to encourage our dog to come out just a
little further, come out just a little further, fresh meat. But we
have survived until October. And we are here now, me and my
husband, building our cabin in the midst of autumn's early
frosts, building now without mosquitoes, building forever in
the hollowness of air that stretches conversation thin. We are
here in the absence of barn swallow clatter, in the absence of
relatives who would have us build another way, who wanted us

to pour cement, who persuaded us to put in those Southern Baptist windows, and who, if they were building a cabin, would have started all over again from scratch. But the weather is through with all of that, and in another night will turn us out, the last of the summer clutter.

So we are stragglers staying on past vacation, past convenience, past our right minds. Nobody wants to be here during hunting season but the hunters. But we are brave. We are lying here on the pine wood floor trying to straighten things out—the twisting in the right shoulder, the contortion in the lower back, the bent-over nails of the entire day. These are our calisthenics. Knees up, hold, rock and hold, stretch again and hold.

Some people would probably think this is funny, but it really is no laughing matter, me lying on my back on the floor of this place, trying to straighten out the curve in my spine. Some people would think it's funny that I'm lying here pretending to rebuild a part of Walden Pond and my back muscles pull me over sideways when I stand up and take a crooked sighting down the barrel of my sister's Luger. But I can't help that. This is where I began, in killing country, in God's country, the worldwide church of God under the pines. We all carry guns here.

My brother Judd carries all kinds—a .22, a .38, a 12-gauge, keeps a pistol in his glove compartment, and belongs to the Black Powder Mountain Rifle Association. He brings stray cats up here to feed to the coyotes, says they can fend for themselves, survival of the fittest and all of that—a regular Wolf Larsen. But Judd blows the hell out of unsuspecting ground squirrels and regales us with uncensored and unsolicited tales of the hunt. This was the buck double-shot while charging, triple-shot as he passed on, and shot again as he disappeared into the brush. This was the buck that walked dazed into the left front fender of my pickup. And this was the buck that surprised us all. But I am not surprised. I have sat up weekends at the end of this barrel, eating Poulsbo bread, sunflower seeds and rye, the bread inspired by God's word (Ezekiel 4:9), and tried to hold firm for the deer. These are killing stories, but I am alive and well and trying to squirm out of the line of fire. Judd says I'm a bleeding hearts liberal, and I don't know what's what. He takes a shot at me for this but misses by a mile, or at least a good yard. And I know that this is not the reason I came up here.

Rather, we came here to build our cabin on terms of antecedent reality, came at the end of digression (it is true), and for future reference, came to lay down our bones on this flat plane to feel the pressure of the past. But we came here for that and something else. I will think of it in a minute.

When my father came here it was to escape his past, the close-quartered sanctity of the religious family order. He moved to northern Idaho because he wanted room to move around, room to raise his family, room to flex his muscles. He became a local legend. Guiding his pack train at risk over the pass into Montana, gyppo logging in the Coeur d'Alenes, and shooting elk and bear out of season whenever he felt like it. But that was the forties, and he was a holdover from another generation, a primitive in settled country, a mountain man in an isolated wilderness stepped over in the mad rush to the sea.

His legend goes like this. One time ole Alton was sitting around this campfire with a bunch of Arkies. They were up blister rusting for the Forest Service and Alton, he was just passing through. So they're sitting there, all these green kids that don't know anything, and they're talking about this and that, and what would they do if a bear came up out of the woods. They're making big plans right and left and finally they begin to get on ole Alton, making fun of his red suspenders or something, and him just sitting there minding his own business. Then kind of casual, Alton speaks up and says this is what he'd do, just pull out his gun real slow; and Alton pulls out his gun real slow; take dead aim; and he raises his pistol to his waist; and shoot; and Alton shoots right between two of them

guys with the biggest mouths and liked to have killed every
guy on that log. Well there was a sudden crash as one boy fell
over backward, and there was a moment or two before they
picked him up and found he was all right before they started
hoorahing Alton again and saying he was a lot of hot air. But
Alton held his ground. And when they stopped jeering, he sat
back down and said quietly, "I think, if you will check, there is
a bear heart-shot right behind you." Well, they checked and
were damned if there wasn't a bear heart-shot dead right behind
them. And that cured them, let me tell you.

Anyway, that's the legend, but I came along much later,
when the mountain man had mellowed and liked to take his
little girl up Bear Creek to chase the bears out of the government dump. We'd go up there in the red jeep and surprise two
or three of them black bears coming up out of the garbage.
Then one time, just for the hell of it, my dad shot one, a small
one, that bawled like a Jersey calf before it died. Killing the bear
was not only illegal, but it was dangerous because of the mother;
and he and my uncle loaded that cub up in a hurry, especially
being in earshot of the ranger station. But no one came around
to ask questions, and back home the bear calf lay on the ground
in front of the house, no visible sign of death, just glazing black
eyes that looked at me almost talking. And when I got down to
take a closer look, my ole man flicked his toes under the head of
that dead bear and growled deep in his throat.

It was only a joke, but the black dumb eyes speak to me yet.
And I think I may remember what that bear looked like better
than I do my father. My father died not much after that, up on
the road across from the house. They found him stretched out
on the bank, reaching up for the tomato soup can he'd just been
shooting at.

That was when I was five, and the Arkies have since run their
dogs all through these woods, and there are hardly any black
bears left. But I keep a lookout for them just the same, and
maybe someday I'll see one.

Anyway, I am here on sacred ground, the center of me, the breath of my effort, rasping away the edges, trying to fit in. And I am here every night, lying cracked up on the floor in the house, my back popping into place like the fire, my mind pulling slivers from the tips of my resistance. We imagine this is Jack London country. We work on the cabin in the day and at night we listen to his stories on cassette—"To Build a Fire," "The Man on Trail," the man with "The One Thousand Dozen," the one immutable idea. This last man, with the eggs, killed himself for an idea while the others merely perished.

And that was it. We are here to form an idea, to flagellate our fingers into submission, to move our arms as if they really were extensions of our brains. And not the other way around—our brains an extension of our arms, cerebral cortex preserved by flexing muscles. We are definitely not here to prove that. But we are here with a concern for the past, I say to myself. What past? I say back. Why do you have concern for this place where your parents survived the depression hand to mouth, where all eight of your brothers and sisters grew up, but you never did, because you came along after Social Security? Why concern for these people who are bonded to you by blood and make interesting pinochle partners, but never heard of the Renaissance? These people who are on the killing side of extinction: the snowy egret and the black-footed ferret, Shakespeare and Frank Lloyd Wright. Concern, I say, because basically, the past is a jumble of happy, remembered lies which someone needs to straighten out. Someone needs to take these people by the throat and lead them in past the Ben Franklin stove and the picture of Christ on the wall and set them down in the middle of the eighties. Someone needs to do it, I say. But I say back to myself, "That's the biggest bunch of bullshit I have ever heard."

So I am nowhere when I thought that I was here. Cutting to length, nailing on my knees, suspended in a paint bucket. I am nowhere. At the bottom of the hole. Talking to rocks. Out there is the woodshed where we used to gut the deer. It intends to be our cabin. But it reels under the weight of the remembered dead, poached deer shot under the moonlight, skinned down to the gun-barrel-blue of the meat. Am I really a part of this? The little girl in Daddy's wallet, in full-length chaps and vest, getting ready for the quick-draw?

I throw out my left arm and try to touch it with my toe. This move is not exactly in the AMA "Guide to a Better Back," but my chiropractor liked it.

Outside, the slaughter shed racks and shudders under our new hammers, twists and groans under the wench and the jack, but always settles back out of kilter. Every wall we build has to be plumbed three ways, two-by-fours shimmed out and chipped in, carved around diagonal logs, and centered on imaginary lines. And when you squint your eyes on a foggy day, it almost looks square, almost looks like something you'd want to live in. But not quite.

The prevailing motif here is rustic, but I came with the idea of creating my own style. My sister's cabin, which is this house, is early yard sale. I'm lying on her latest addition—Indian Aztec throw rugs. On the walls, she has a cracked antique chamber pot from England, two tin lanterns that don't work, a clothespin rocking chair, and a cowboy with a red bandanna over his chipped nose. She's out of work but manages every weekend to bring another piece of junk up here. Her theory is this: she keeps nothing in her cabin worth taking, so she'll have nothing there to steal.

Judd's barn is more traditional, late primitive—coats hanging from elk horns on the left, two-man saw in the middle, Earth stove in the corner, four singletrees overhead, and coats hanging from elk horns on the right. But he has the advantage of logs. Before his cabin was the barn, it was a forest ranger station. Someone took it apart, log by log, numbered them along the seam in the corner with Silas Lapham paint that'd last forever and put it back together right there. Judd resurrected it five years ago and built it into a fort. Says the only way anyone's getting into his place is with a chain saw.

Then there is us. Our cabin is not so much the way we

wanted it, as much as it is the way things are turning out. I had in mind something more like a writer's retreat, the kind of place you could walk into wearing a smoking jacket, something one with the land, living quarters suspended over running water. I see now there is too much dead wood lying around here for that. What we have out there jacked up on cement blocks is something more like borrowed time, living quarters suspended over the debris of the past. A cabin, one with nothing. When you stand back to get the full view, it looks more like a cathedral with flying buttresses, used lumber and yard sale doors jutting out from the sides, the architectural design wavering between gothic simplicity and gingerbread classic. I'll never forgive my sister for talking me into the trim across the front and that front window. Judd's brother-in-law had these glass panels five feet long and they were cheap, and Judd and Eileen said they would be easy to install, and to make a long story short, guess where they ended up after an entire week's figuring and measuring and wondering if they were going to fit between the eaves. Anyway they are in and they are elegant. The morning light streams in just about the time a famous novelist would want to sleep in. But I'm not complaining. I've gotten free advice before and some of it was good.

Basically though, I have to say this. There is something out there coming together. We like to call it our cabin. But it reminds us of something else.

It is eleven o'clock. The fire is roaring in Mother's old Ashley and all the doors and windows are open. Denton finishes his situps, but I think I'll pass on mine tonight. This floor is killing me. Denton goes into the kitchen to turn off the propane. We lie in bed waiting for the lights to go out. Yes, we have made it this far. We are gratified. Tomorrow we can go back to town and develop our film and lie down on our warm waterbed and think back on how much we miss this place. Denton, hanging by a rope on the roof; me, pretending to hold up the corner of the cabin; Denton, bending over until his underwear shows;

and me, with my nose pressed against the glass. The lights go out.

We listen to Radio Havana Cuba on the shortwave for a little while, "Stay out of Nicaragua, you white capitalistic swine," and then I turn it off. Finally we are alone with our thoughts, the crackling of the fire, the faint whiff of propane and Bengay, and the promise that tomorrow we will be back in Smog City with a real toilet. But Denton says he hears something. He always hears something. We could be a mile underground and he would still hear something. We lie listening. Could it be possible that the house is still settling after all these years? The fire pops and the wood shifts with a bang against the metal. Then we see it—the quick flash of light and shadow against the wall. There is a car coming up the canyon. We roll over and lift ourselves up on our hands to look out the window. We see nothing. The light has gone into a ravine.

Judd said that he and his boys were hunting last year and came across an abandoned campsite up Callus Creek, five miles from here. He found groceries, garbage, and gear, and a Chevy truck that looked like it had been through a war but would probably still run. He said it looked like there hadn't been anybody there for weeks, and when they were looking around to see if anybody needed help and if he still wanted his sleeping bag, found the Aryan nation information in the glove compartment. Figured it belonged to that guy they had just arrested, and he had been camping out in our back yard.

There are the lights again, coming around the point where the apple tree has been trying to grow for a hundred years. The lights move slowly, flickering through the Douglas fir along the road. Denton says he can hear the ping of the rocks under the tires. We wonder who it could be at this time of night. Nobody ever goes by at this time of night. Then the car is out of the trees and moves across the base of Deer Hill, across the flat directly in front of the house. It's moving slowly, too slowly. Then it stops. Damn, they're checking us out.

Denton reaches toward the night stand and ends up knocking the aspirin bottle onto the floor; it hits like a rattle. I am next to the wall and can't move. "What are you doing?"

Denton says, "Where's the bullets? Where's the damn bullets?" But we are saved. The car starts moving again. It disappears across our window, into the trees on the left through more Doug fir, flickering out of sight around the bend. Denton turns on the flashlight and sticks the gun back in the holster. "Boy was that a close one."

I lie next to the wall and don't move. "Do you mean to tell me you were actually going to load that gun? You had it out of the holster ready for the O.K. Corral and everything? Wait'll I tell Eileen." Denton turns out the light and rolls back on the bed, rebuffed.

"Get serious," he says.

But how can I get serious? All this is a big joke. Judd says they probably wouldn't come in outright and start shooting. Would you risk it? Open up fire before you knew what you had to deal with? No, they probably wouldn't operate like that. First they would come in here quiet and ask for a wrench or something to fix their motorbikes. And wouldn't you give it to them, you being stranded so far from civilization and them standing around and not willing to leave until you give it to them? And if some guy asked for gasoline, wouldn't you give it to him, showing him how to siphon your underground tank, content in knowing that he doesn't know where you've hidden your two-bit Mickey Mouse key? And wouldn't you do some other idiot thing to show how vulnerable you were because the guy is friendly enough, and because you wouldn't want the freak to get mad and come back with a shotgun? You would do it. Give him any damn thing he wanted. And as soon as he had the lay of things, how many men, how many women, and how many guns, do you think it would be long? Do you think they would hesitate for one minute? And Carol Rose says at this point, "But who would want this place, when you can see it from the road?" And Eileen says here, "You couldn't fortify it. You couldn't hold it." And I say, "That makes sense. They'd pick off those cabins up Short Creek first. You could hole up in the mouth of that box canyon for years. That is until they brought in air support." And we all get a good laugh at that sitting there eating chips and dip.

Then Denton and I hear it at the same time—the bounce of car springs on that first big bump as you turn off the main road down our lane. Denton says, "You think I should load the gun now?" I say, "Sure."

The car emerges from the trees with its lights off. This is it. We've had it. The dark, malignant form makes a sharp left past our cabin, turns broadside toward the house. Our pickup? Don't they see our pickup? No, we parked it behind the shed so we could load up our tools and go home. They don't see it. They don't think anyone is here. Then they stop in front of the house, a van, the engine whining high with an idle problem. Denton is still fumbling with the gun. "Did you get it?" I pant.

"One bullet," he says.

We keep watching the van out the window, try to keep our faces away from the glass, but try to keep the van in view. We corral it with our eyes and watch for emerging forms. The fire cracks again. The fire. Can't they see our smoke? We can see theirs—the tailpipe exhaust in the cold and a pinprick of light up front in the cab—a cigarette, one light, then two. Denton says, "What are we going to do?" I say, "Make a noise, scare 'em." Instead he turns on the flashlight, shines it on the pistol grip of the .45 and says, "Where's the damn safety?" And that is enough. The engine revs and throttles down, lurches around in a circle, and disappears down the road in a trail of moonlit dust. Whoever it was did not want to tangle with Denton and his .45. I try to sleep with the image of the disappearing van still in my head, but the Rock Falls dust, thick from the poundings of a dry summer, remains suspended, infinitely filtering.

In the late August morning when we wake up, there is nothing left of the moonlight adventure. The petunias in the window boxes hang heavy with frost. The ground is almost white. Even the grass breaks under our feet. The dust is frozen solid in crystallized patterns of mud. So we lock up. We lap over the shutters on our shed, the ones we bolted together out of parts of Mother's old barn in town, the heavy parts. We lap them over and wedge them tight from the inside. We padlock them where nobody can reach. Security locks on security hinges, on each of the three doors it took four people to carry and 92 bolts, 115 screws, 17 railroad spikes, and a pound of nails to hold in place. Not enough to stop a bullet but enough to stop a high-powered interest. Then suddenly it hits us, the bolted doors underneath and the glass windows overhead, the unshutterable windows someone talked us into building, built so wide there's no room for anything to shutter and fold back. We have been pretending about them, that they weren't really a threat because they don't open and they aren't on the ground level. Who could reach them? What would be the point? The point is this—the perfect target! Five vertical panes reaching to the peak, a challenge, an enticement, a compulsion. This morning the five panes are etched with frost and reflect the morning light like prisms. And then it hits me again, the motif, not yard sale classic or neo-Medieval, but modern—Modern Rustic in fact—an open invitation from the road. Not exactly what I had in mind when we began. I tell Denton. We stand shellshocked in a world that will go silent tomorrow. A bunch of civilized nonsense in the middle of idiocy. So we are going home, and may not be back for a year. And here this place will be, empty, quiet, alluring. The glint of intelligence in the eye of dumb nature. Some place to draw a bead.

But even if the neo-Nazis don't find us and the insane hunters fail to beat a path through our door, there is something else in the air. It grabs you by the shoulders and shakes you. It pinches your face and whacks you on the side of the head. It goes for your throat. It is the overwhelming idea of the tree in the forest, falling or not falling, the quintessential absence of sound. It is the idea of this—the cleared space of land that was once home ground, but is now the cluttering valley of our three cabins, this cleared space of land, the picture of it, the morning fog lifting in the darkened canyon trench on a visible world going white, going flash-white, mute-white, blank—the flurry of hammers blotted out.

SIDE EFFECTS

My mother is wrapping a phantom string around my hand. Her fingers pinching like duck bills, she pantomimes this unreality in the air above her bed, this gathering and endless wrapping of string around my hand. I hold my arm across the rail, awkward, hold it there because she has my thumb. With one hand she has my thumb and with the other she pulls more string from beneath the covers, pinches it and pokes it until she finds the end. Then she lays it against the ball already forming and begins again, around and around, until my hand is tight.

This is her drug-induced hallucination, this constant winding of string. It is the mind working through unresolved reality, working by force of habit against this new condition, by force of will against sedation, by force of boredom against time.

It is the complete essence of personality in a ravel. Holding my arm through the rail, I sit beside the living room bed, watching this subconscious world we like to keep under wraps. I want to abstract it, objectify it, experiment on it, dissect it until there is not one shred of evidence left. I want to make this an investigation into the side effects of bone cancer.

The cancer itself is obscure. The side effects of radiation are these: loss of hearing, loss of appetite, disorientation, and loss of feeling in the extremities. The side effects of chemotherapy are these: loss of hearing, loss of appetite, loss of hair, and loss of feeling in the extremities.

But the experiment itself does not want to be objective. It is my mother, the one who brought in other people's laundry and said she didn't have the time, but who spread her blue-veined legs against the linoleum floor and drew a chalk circle between us, so that I could be the first female marble champion of the fifth grade. She lies before me now, her face fixed and intent, and she seems to be unaware that I am here, except for my hand, which she pulls into position, pulls it up when it droops so that she can pass her hand underneath.

For weeks this has been her hallucination, the salvaging of string, of yarn, of thread, of floss. The county nurse says the hallucinations are an uncontrollable side effect of the morphine. And the doctor says that mental aberrations are a natural consequence of the cancer. Mother says, "Hold your arm still. Do like I tell you," and I lean harder into the rail.

This is the way many of us handle it, my sister Eileen, my brother Judd, and his wife Carol Rose, all of us leaning into the rail to make our mother as comfortable as possible. But we are not without our moments, our passing fits of levity. We are the home team, the affiliated stations, the ones who empty the bedpans and bring you live from her living room, Mother and her flying fingers.

I try to flex my hand to relieve the cramp in my arm, but she pulls back on my thumb.

The winding of string, however, is only what's on the front

burner for today. It is all part of a greater domestic whole. We have always been great quilters in this family, the women. It comes with the territory. It is inevitable, like knots in old yarn, clabber in sour milk. So we sit here in the living room at Hayden Lake, Mother in the bed quilting and winding madly, my sister and sister-in-law and I in rotation, (and incidentally Judd, a misfit in the great chain of being), sitting beside the bed holding our hands just so, so as not to disturb the way she sees things.

This is her apocalyptic view of the order of the universe, women pulling a measure from a basket. Together this past Christmas, we bought over two hundred dollars worth of new material, new material in spite of the cancer, quilting material to be folded and cut into perfect and useless squares. Just two months ago I cut twelve new quilts, shaded them into pastels, after experimenting with gray and black, cut just enough to keep her busy until my next vacation. They sit in their boxes now, out on the shelves, queen-size pink, twin blue-brown, double lavender.

And this is the way things have been arranged for us sinners in the quilting bee of life. How many years have I labeled quilt boxes? How many years a conscientious objector? I am the youngest, the tractable one, the one who comes home on weekends to take care of her mother, the one who has always sacrificed vacation to the will of her mother. I am the youngest and the furthest from pioneer stock, the one who forgets Edith Wharton and Virginia Woolf for granny squares. But I cannot forget this—that all our lives we have been cramming everything in between the stitches, and that this last Christmas vacation, in particular, was only an upgraded episode in the frantic factory momentum of piecework, the rushed scissor-click before the bell.

We sat there at Christmas, across the table from one another, clicking away madly, trying to cram all our lives into the straight-line succession of one week's days. And we almost made it. There was only that one slip, one poke of the needle that drew blood, that sent me to the basement sulking over the time it cost me to cut out those quilts, and sulking over having to listen at the same time to the praise of my older brother Judd, who is here when I can't be to bring in the wood, who is here when I can't be to start the fire, who is here when I can't be, to put it out.

And this is the way things have been arranged now: when we brought Mother home from the hospital, we arranged to take care of her ourselves, in her own home, as they say. And things being what they are in other parts of the world, it was arranged that the two of us would be together on this weekend. It is my temporary experience with Mother, my weekend trips from school, my charity in her behalf.

In the mornings, I try to make an impression with breakfast. I pour a dribble of juice into the glass. I dilute the cream-of-wheat. I butter the half-toasted toast, sink the table knife into the shell of a steaming egg, and scrape the jell into a crystal saucer. I juggle this on a tray into the living room by Mother's bed. We pretend to have breakfast. We do not eat much. Mother sips at the cream-of-wheat, nudges the toast into the egg, pours her grapefruit juice onto the tray. She makes her own impression.

But we are all on a great diet here. It's a contest. The couple who loses the least amount of weight by July has to take the others out to dinner. We have great diet dinners together and face each dieting face across the table and trade dieting success stories. We are paired like this: my husband and I, Judd and Carol Rose, and Judd again with Eileen because Eileen is divorced and needs a partner. But Eileen says she is going to weigh in with Mother as her partner instead of Judd. It is her great dieting joke about Mother, who has lost forty pounds in two months since Christmas and will never make it to July, about Mother, whose private irony it is to live so long on stored energy.

It is a private irony and our in-house dieting joke. Some of us, the other parts of this family, men and women, do not understand such humor. They come to the house with their long faces not really wanting to know what goes on here. They want rosy cheeks and covered bedpans, a bathrobe and a full set of teeth. We have to take care of them as well as Mother. They come dragging their own dying behind them, I suppose, these people, up and down the hall, and only retire to the kitchen when they are ready to rally around themselves and tell you about peach cobbler. You could kill them for this, the brown sugar dripping, the top slightly crusted. But instead you hold your water glass up to your eye and disarrange their faces.

So they go on and tell you their stories, and you go on and tell them yours. And when they are through melting all over themselves, you sweep them out the door, and they say to you with their eyes, How can you stand to live in the same house with a crazy person?

In any case, we have to hide our diet food from the un-discriminating and ask them to eat out. But to be fair, we keep other things from them. It is our private conspiracy. We say, "She had a bad night last night," or "She's doing a little better today. The medication keeps the pain down." And they seem satisfied with that and never ask, "What is it really like?" It is only in the inner circle that any of the truth makes sense any-way. If you were to say to them that sometimes Mother re-gresses, you'd only have to explain that sometimes she thinks she is a child. That is, you'd have to say, sometimes she sticks her fingers into her glass. That is, she spills it and embarrasses us. That is, when you try to stop her, she recoils and cries for her mommy to make us stop teasing her. Can I really tell them this, these people who only know appearances, these people who are too trapped in the past of her to see the present of her?

So we keep other things from them, the morphine sup-positories, the nightly maneuvers, the milligrams of this, the fluid ounces of that, the time she lost her imaginary scissors in-side the bed and tore out all the sheets and ripped out their hems trying to find them. We record these privileges but keep our faith inside a sealed jar beside the bed.

Mother squeezes my hand like I am not paying attention, and I lift it back into its proper place.

The observable data tell me this: we are all balancing a crystal saucer on a jiggling tray. At night when we converge for our diet dinners there is a consensus. We tell our funny stories like this: Jackie came down today. She walked into the living room to say hello, just normal, and Mother looked up kind of funny and said, "Who do you think you look like?" And Jackie said, laughing, "I look like me." And Mother said, "Who in the hell told you that?"

Or we might say: "You know how Mother wakes up not knowing where she is sometimes. Well, one day I came in and she was just staring at the light fixture on the ceiling. Just staring. And I say, 'Mother, is there something wrong?' And she laughs and comes back to where I am and says, 'You know that light has saved me many a time,'" which means she looked up and saw the familiar gold wires crisscrossed underneath, and she knew where she was because she has always hated that fixture.

Or we tell the one about the train. One day Mother woke up screaming. "Eileen, get me out of here." "But Mother," Eileen told her, "you're in bed. You can't get up, remember?" And Mother putting two and two together says, "Well, move my bed then; there's a train a-coming."

Or we tell the one about playing cards like the one I will tell about the string. It is all great fun, though some stories are funnier than others.

I hold Mother's hands, the hands writers like to describe as talons, useless bony things of prey. I counted this three times in one month, in Welty, in Cather, in O'Connor, people who should know better. I ask Mother, "What on earth do you plan to do with all this string?" She says, "I don't know."

Once Eileen brought in some playing cards, two decks, mixed, upside down and sideways. She brought these to Mother who was propped up in bed over her food tray. Eileen

says, "See what I found. A mess of cards the kids or somebody's been playing with," and she flops them onto the tray.
She knew what she was doing. I thought it was rude, an insult
to my mother's former intelligence. But Mother picked up the
cards, looked at the familiar rose pattern on the back and went
to work, her talon hands pinching the cards off the talon stack.
And when she finished with that, Eileen handed her another
pile and another, until Eileen got tired of messing them up.
Then they played solitaire, Eileen leaning over the table, suggesting that a two goes on the three and Mother suggesting
that the four card was missing from that deck, she was pretty
sure, so a five would do just as well. All of which made you
wonder about how easy it was for her to cheat, and about all
those times playing pinochle, canasta, and crazy eights.

At lunch I open a can of soup, heat it in the microwave, drop
the sections of mandarin orange into the cottage cheese, pour
half a glass of milk, and butter a bread. We have lunch. That is,
I carry the tray into the living room—full, and then I carry it
back—full, because Mother insists that we just had breakfast
and that I am trying to pull a fast one.

Going along is usually the safest, but there are no guarantees.
Like one time in particular when I came late to give her breakfast, and she was fumbling with her hands beneath the covers.
She looked at me funny, her eyes someone else's eyes, and she
said, "What are you going to do about this puppy?" A puppy? I
came in to give her breakfast; what was I supposed to do with a
puppy? She folded back the covers and told me to look, her fingers kneading the folded blanket. "Get this puppy out of here.
He doesn't belong in here."

"A puppy?" I said. "Where did you get a puppy?" Her answer was quick, perfectly logical. "Harmon brought him."
Harmon, her brother-in-law and my uncle, who comes on his
deathbed visits, comes out of her southern Idaho farming past,
a seventy-year-old man, to make teenage chauvinist jokes about
women. "A puppy?" I said. "Yes. Take him outside where he

belongs." She has always had this thing about animals being in the house. But it was Harmon who brought this puppy, and it was me who had to deal with it.

So I tried to please her, but there simply was no puppy. "There's a puppy in here, honest. You've got to believe me." So I grabbed the imaginary puppy and took him into the kitchen, but when I came back, instead of repose, I found her confused and angry. "Who do you think you're trying to fool? Take this puppy!" "Mother," I said, I would tell her anything but this: "There is no puppy." "No puppy?" "No puppy. It's the medication. It tricks you and makes you see things." She lay quietly for a moment. "No puppy, really?" "Really." Her arms relaxed back against the bed, and she looked around, resigned her gaze to the ceiling and said, "Where's my breakfast, or was that a trick too?"

Sometimes at dinner, Eileen will say some scatterbrained thing. It is usually Eileen, and there will be a moment of hesitation, of recognition, and Carol Rose with her big mouth will say, "Been into the morphine again, deary?" Then it is all over, the pretense we make of making sense, and the great game of who-is-most-like-Mother begins.

"Seen any trains lately?"

"Not in the last five minutes, but I'll let you know."

This is, of course, slightly irreverent. I realize that. It is also postnasal drip of the mind, phlebitis of the liver, and constipation of the heart. But Mother understands. We speak the same language. She says, "If you don't hold your hand like I tell you, I'm going to beat your brains out."

I ask how much longer is this going to take, and she says, "Until I'm done."

At night beside the bed, waiting for Mother to ring the cowbell, I drift in and out of sleep. I sleep in the living room with Mother because I cannot hear from my old room. I sleep lightly because of my growing deafness, the hereditary hardening of the inner ear. In spite of calcification, I lie listening to the refrigerator kick a load of ice into the tray, listening to the water in the pipes in the hall, listening to breathing.

At intervals I dream. I take the cat out into the night, under the street light of parked humpbacked Dodges, old Dodges in front of a closed store where I planned to take my cat to dinner. But it's a closed store, guarded by Ninja in the night, who follow me to where we live, my cat and I. And they try to climb the chain link fence that keeps them out, try to climb it, but I hose them down just in time. But the fence is not chain link after all; it is old barn wood with orange lichen growing on it, like the picture frame around my cat, and I have the barn wood; it is around my place. Mother gave me the barn wood and all is safe, the barn wood gate I climbed to feed the cows, the barn wood gate wet with water where the Ninja climb, their nails digging in soft rotten barn wood.

But when I am awake, it strikes me that we sold the barn wood last year, at least that part of Mother's place where the fence and gate lie buried in the grass.

It is a trivial dream, a minor adjustment. Dreams like these are the least of our troubles. Recurring dreams are another matter. With these there is more time for interpretation. It has always been the tradition in this family that the men should do the killing, perhaps with the exception of chickens. So it is, when the dog gets hit by a car, when the calves are ready for slaughter, it is the man's job to end life. I suppose because such things are supposed to be beyond the ability of women. Maybe they are right. In my nightmare the dog gets hit by a car and I am alone. I have to kill the dog, my German Shepherd named Pup, who lies in the gravel kicking in blood. So using my baseball bat, I begin my dutiful drubbing, but the dog won't die because I can't hit hard enough. And just when I learn how much strength it takes to cave in the skull, I realize the dog could have been saved. I thought I would be surprised by death, but have come to find out I've known about it for some time.

Yesterday when some of the relatives from the outer circle

came to the house, Mother called them to her side with the slight motion of her hand. She called to them and pulled them down to confide, "I think these people are trying to kill me." And that is what it's all about really. Like my sister working double shifts, first an eight-hour day at the plastic plant, then nights here, jumping to the cowbell and then the alarm, an eternity of waking. Never having time to spend one night at her own home, listening to her whining terrier, the old whining terrier who is past her pup-bearing years, who had her last batch of them five years ago. Just enough time to yell at the whining dog and threaten to put her out, but locking her in the bathroom instead, so that both of them could sleep. But whining still, and yelping at the last, until suddenly stopping, and then there on the bathroom floor one wet terrier puppy. One life only in the litter, but one life still, plopped into the toilet and flushed away before there was time for anyone to develop the idea of mourning.

Mother twists my thumb until it hurts. I pull it back because it is my thumb after all. "Wait just a minute," she says. "I'm almost done." I have trouble believing I'll soon have my thumb back. I nudge the metaphor, the one that defines the way she must move her hands. "You'll have to finish soon," I say, "because I have to feed the cats." These are four growing cats one generation away from wild, cats we stand in the bathtub to see, to get just a glimpse out of the window of wild uninhibited cat, Mother's wild cats, which we sometimes trick with old shoelaces into almost being able to touch. "I have to go feed our cats," I say.

She makes a knot. It is an indication I've said something that makes sense and that there may soon be relief for my arm stretched out and cramped. She makes three more giant passes around my fingers and catches at the ends, pulls two more knots down hard, and looks out at me satisfied. We stare at each other momentarily, poised on the edge of uncertainty, hesitating for just a second, afraid we may not have seen the same things. Then, suddenly, it is me who has not understood. Who is taking care of whom? I am seeing my mother in her flights of fantasy, for the first time—a string in one hand, my thumb in the other, trying to tie up a few loose ends. I have been in college too long. I have read too many unnecessary things. She pushes my hand toward the rail, one of those go-on-do-like-I-tell-you shoves, and says, "There! Take that out to the cat dish."

So I stand slowly, shifting the strain in my right shoulder, letting the cramps work out of my legs, testing the floor with the pins in the balls of my feet. I hold my weighted hand over the bed, palm up, waiting for change. I let her see what I am doing. With my free hand I pull the covers up over her arms, the pink sheet, the flowered blanket, the thermal spread. I tell her she should rest now. There has been too much quilting around here for one day. But she, her hands folded properly beneath the blanket, betrays a field of paisley behind her eyes. And I move my wrapped hand away, carrying the illusion, holding it out in front of me into the kitchen—a giant ball of string for the domesticating cats.

HOUSE PAINTING DEAL

I'm sitting here stirring paint. Stirring paint in the house my mother built. This is the house that she built after the old man died. Built and lived in for twenty-nine years, but empty now, empty except for the pile of junk waiting by the door for the Salvation Army. It was Mother's junk, junk she has been hoarding since the last World War. Junk we cleaned out after her funeral. It's all good stuff, too good to throw away because it was Mother's, but junk all the same because it has no useful value to the rest of us.

So it is Mother's junk. It has all come down to this last pile, one last mountain range to be moved—plastic flowers stapled to wire mesh frames, a rooster wall plaque with half the beans missing, and one dusty bluebird sitting askew inside a fake coat hanger cage. And rag-rug material. There is enough rag-rug material to cover the floor of George Washington's White House, rag-rug material rolled up into tight woolly balls, balancing precariously around the mountain's perimeter in garbage sacks. And don't forget the prehistoric dresses that I have never seen anybody wear.

All this stuff sits on the far side of the room between the door and the front window. It is the last of the loot, the last of the cleaning, the last of accumulation. We never thought that we would get to the end of it, to the bottom of everything. But there it is. The last of an unclaimed inheritance. And now I can finish painting this place, collect my money for passing Go, and get the hell out of here.

The situation is this. They have left me the refrigerator, a mattress and box springs, one chair, and the phone. In case the real estate agent calls. As if I had time to talk to a real estate agent with a paint roller in my hand. Why can't Eileen take care of that after I leave, after the paint has dried? As if they ever thought of me. Little sister. It would suit me fine if they would just leave me alone for two weeks, leave me alone instead of coming over here to "help." Every time Eileen comes over, she expects to set the world straight inside of ten minutes. And every time she comes over, she breaks something in less than five. She tightens a loose screw and breaks the storm window on the front door. Changes a light bulb and throws the circuit breaker. Zaps over just in time to back into fresh paint. This is how she is helping me. I try to tell her I work best alone, but she pries off the old thermostat and leaves a gaping hole in the wallboard. And I have to fix that too.

So far, I have found it is difficult to work with a sister. I never knew that before. My brothers and sisters were all older. Another generation. Out to lunch. I never had to put up with them until now. It's a sad situation. Sad but true. I never knew I had brothers and sisters until it came down to dividing the loot.

Get this picture—my brother Jarvis, closest to me but older, his wife, his seven kids, all going in different directions through

my mother's house on a dead run. That's nine pairs of arms
reaching into cupboards and pulling out popcorn poppers.
That's eighteen individual feet padding down the stairs and
dragging things up from the basement. And that's ninety fingers and opposable thumbs closing around Mother's animal
knickknacks she and I bought at the San Diego Zoo. That's
ninety digitals closing around our shared past and cramming it
into overstuffed garbage bags. Do you get the picture now?
The bedroom door slamming back, the sounds of "Hey, look
what I found," as someone, someone older, pulls the last of the
extra bedding down from the top shelf of *our* bedroom closet.

You never do get used to it, the "sharing," sitting there in the
kitchen where you thought you could be objective, sitting
there cringing against the slam of the back door screen and
bracing yourself against the steady rhythm of flailing arms and
swinging keesters. It all goes by you and around you, and you
can only marvel at what ten-year-old fingers want. There goes
that kid of Jarvis's. Watch him blitz past and grab a potholder
out of the hands of his kissing cousin. See her lash back ver-
bally. That girl has feminist potential. See it all transpire. When
you are objective, you can marvel at yourself for marveling at
what ten-year-old fingers want. That is, you can marvel until
you've seen the family silver trotting out the back door. Then
everything collapses around you because you know. You know
that this kid of Jarvis's is a chip of a chip off the old block—the
kid, my brother Jarvis, and our old man.

"Our old man," we always called him. Because after his heart
attack when he was thirty, he was prematurely old. "The old
man" to all of his children, but "Alton" to anybody who ever
worked for him. And "son-of-a-bitch" to anybody who
ever worked against him. That was our old man the time that
hauler came down to the house to look at the books. "I got a
right to see them books. I got a right to see the figures." He
was worried about the old man's math, about how many log
feet he'd actually hauled out of the mountains and about how

many he'd actually been paid for. "He said it was all written down in his books, and I want to see them." The hauler stood there beside his empty rig, the sawdust and sweat sticking to his face like a beard. He'd come to the house knowing the old man wouldn't be there, knowing he'd still be in the woods. And he stood there in his rage saying, "I got a right to see them figures." But *we* didn't know what books he was talking about, "we" in the sense of our remembered family consciousness, in the sense that this was the story I was told. We didn't know the old man kept any books. We had never seen any. And the hauler had climbed into the rig thinking that we were all in on it together, in on the plot to skim the profits off the haulers.

And now it has come down to this—the coda to this logging scenario. When last week we were going through Mother's cedar chest, the place where she kept all the secret secrets—the birth certificates and yellowed report cards—we found our father's ledger. The one long green government account book that at one time had belonged to the Forest Service, but had become "Property of Alton J. Sanderson." And there it was, the official record at last, suddenly unearthed from the dust of the catacombs, and we sat there waiting, me and another brother, Judd, who happened by, sat there waiting while Eileen flipped through the pages, waiting to find out if after all these years, the hauler had really been justified. "Well?" we said. "Is that the book or isn't it?"

She toyed with us for half a minute, this sister pushing fifty, but still the primal sister with our lives in the palms of her hands. She toyed with us for half a minute and then finally relented and said, "No, I don't think so." And she half turned the green ledger around and fanned the pages in our faces. "So there," she said. "Just a blank." And as she said the words, had we felt the full weight of her vindication? Did we still know who the boss was around here? But then, as she flipped through the ledger, there really was something on one of the pages, something written under "S." Judd and I saw it at the same time. And we both paged back with her, fumbling at the yellow dog-eared pages that were completely blank but somehow worn. And then there it was. It was the old man's logging record after all. But such a record. Only one entry, one quickly scrawled entry that seemed to hesitate on the very page— "Sanderson Timber, April Logs, white pine 1040, spruce 22,610, tamarack 8800, fir 660." No remarks. No context. No incoming. No outgoing. Only the figures for April. And before that and after that—silence.

But what did this mean? Did this mean the old man was "gyppo logging" after all, and creaming his profits off the haulers? Is that what it meant when they called him "gyppo logger," when they said it in their back-slapping voices? Or did it merely indicate that "writing it down" was the devil's game and that any fool could keep the figures in his own head? Had he started to keep a record then changed his mind? Or had he just gotten lazy? But there were the figures for April. Big numbers for little heads. Why not write it all down? So that no one would forget? Where was the danger in that? What did he have to hide? And then, a kind of understanding passed between us, a kind of familial understanding that is only possible between siblings, between Eileen, and Judd, and myself. The old man *had* been keeping two sets of records. There was the proof on the blank page, except for the entry under "S." And all those phantom records, the incoming and the outgoing, accounts payable and accounts receivable, had been added in his head. And each of us, knowing our old man, knew what that added up to.

And that was the pattern before they threw away the mold. The old man before he died, the archetypal sinner. Subsequently, there has been a diminution of the gene pool, a petty ante illustration of the type. Take ten parts old man, one part Mother, and there you have it—Jarvis!

Jarvis, trading you out of your air rifle, making you a real good deal, swapping you two things for one—his gas-powered airplane and transistor radio for your air rifle. A real good deal.

As long as you didn't try to run anything. "Needs some work," he said. Like a new engine and maybe a transistor or two. And there is Jarvis, after you've traded your air rifle, the one you gathered beer bottles all summer to buy, there is Jarvis out in the field shooting the gophers that should have been yours.

All this makes you wonder how you ever ended up on the wrong end of a deal like that. It's a lot like wondering how you ended up on the deal of painting the house. But let's not go into that. That's the way deals in this family go. It sounded like the right thing to do at the time, make peace with the past by scraping every board and laying down a fresh coat of paint. It was me they thought of first, knew I would fall for the sentimental pitch. So here I am stirring paint.

Stirring paint by hand is a delicate operation. You'd like to go fast to hurry the thing, but if you do, you only slop it over the sides. You have to dig with your stick through the caked pigment on the bottom of the can, and then you have to swirl it in slow. It's the only way when nobody left you a bigger bucket, one of those five gallon soap buckets Mother used to have a million of. Yes, one of those soap buckets you saw stuffed full of cake mixes being lugged out the kitchen door. When you don't have one of those buckets, you have to do it this way. Dig on the bottom and swirl it in, letting the stick gently scrape the sides. It's a lost art, what else can I say? They are not paying me by the hour.

This place belonged to Mother. The ranch was the old man's, but this place in town was hers. A rib of the ranch, made out of lumber milled on our land, tamarack and Doug fir skidded from the center of the earth, brought down from Rock Falls in small truck loads until it was all piled house-high and unshaven behind the barn. A place for catching grasshoppers, a sliver patch for bare palms.

It was the house she built after the old man died. Took the lumber to Spokane herself to have it planed, took it over in three loads on the International truck, the red truck, before it was sold. But that was always the way it was when it came to caring about a house, when it came to being choosey about the place where you would live. She had to look out for the babies, think of rats climbing into the flour, but he had to look out for the money.

That's why they bought this place, because the price was right, because the old floors were eaten through with dry rot. A real bargain. And that's why she wanted to rebuild. She had him nearly convinced at one time, when the money was coming in, when the logging was at its peak, before the old man died. And after he was gone, she went ahead with her plans. But it was, by then, a metamorphosed plan. It was, "the way he would have wanted it." So she built her house. The house she had always been planning to build, after moving from one rat-trap rental to another, any available rat-trap rental that was big enough to fit so many kids.

So Mother built this house, tore down the dry rotted floors and walls, poured the cement, laid the brick, spackled every wall I run my roller over. The boys and my sister, Eileen, built this house, this house that the real estate agent says will be hard to sell. It is the worst kind, the kind where somebody did it themselves.

And my room, that's the worst of all. Turquoise paint. That's the worst kind. Nobody buys a house with a turquoise room. It took three coats of beige to paint over my old room. If the real estate lady only knew how I talked to get that blue room in the first place. "A blue room would be too cold," my mother said. That was before we added central heating. Too cold, she said. So we compromised on olive green. I nearly got frostbite in olive green. The second time around I got turquoise blue. She was tired of my whining. And this time, the last time, it took three coats of all-purpose beige to hide that blue, and still the tint bleeds through in a kind of compromise light green. And that's what the real estate lady said, that turquoise won't sell.

I've seen some do-it-yourselfers use a rotor on the end of a drill to mix the paint. But that's so messy. It's like using an egg-beater when all you really need is a spoon. Then somebody's got to clean up. And with paint, it's not like you can lick the beaters. The point is, anything you put into the paint other than a stick you have to clean. And what, may I ask, have they left here for me to clean with? No, this is the best way—slow and steady.

So red paint! Now that was a story. When the old man bought red paint for the racks on his truck. He liked red. "What did you go and buy red paint for?" she said, as if she didn't know already that it wasn't for the house. Not one thing for the house since they had been married. Not one thing wherever they were living, southern Idaho, Bayview, Linfore, Pritchard. Not one thing to make a house more livable. No curtains, no carpets, no nothing.

"It's good paint," he said.

They were living at the ranch at the time, my brother Jarvis picking up slivers in his knees from the wood floors. "What did you buy red paint for, when we really needed linoleum?" speaking of it, then, already in the past tense, like she would never get another chance. "Didn't you think to get us a piece of linoleum?" It reminded them both of the time before, in a house in southern Idaho, when she had bought a piece of linoleum off the truck of a traveling linoleum man. Paid for it out of the food money. Bought just one scrap of linoleum to put on the floor because of one of the kids, bought just one piece of linoleum that the old man gave her hell for.

"Why did you buy a scrap like that, when I would have got you some better?" They both remembered. "It's good paint," the old man said, "for my truck." And he put the can of paint on the shelf, and it stayed there for nearly a month before he used it on the floor. Painted the kitchen floor enamel red and took care of the slivers. Pink diapers, but no slivers. Painted the floor red enamel to shut her up, but made her madder than hell.

That was red paint, but this here that I'm mixing is blue. A half-full can I found under the stairs. It sticks in the bottom real good. You have to stir it a long time.

I have found all kinds of things in the basement like this, things that everyone else has passed up, things of little value. And I have found surprises. Like when I pulled the built-ins out, slid out the drawers so that I could paint behind. That's where I found the missing pool ball, the number five, and sent it along to Jarvis so that he could put it with his set. That's where I found the number five, where no one else had looked. It's been behind there a long time, since one of the grandkids "put" it there. How they managed that, I'll never know.

But the grandkids are always losing pool balls. That's the name of the game. See who can shoot it across the table and get it to jump off. If you hit just right, on the corner by the pocket, they jump off and roll under something. It's all great fun. What else would you expect from the children of siblings? That missing five is the reason we had two sets, one set for kids and one for adults, hidden in the top drawer of the oak buffet, the one they used to shut a sock on to keep me out of. But later we got a key. Jarvis figured out how to make a key in junior high just so he could keep people out, have one drawer that his little sister wasn't poking her nose into. And after that we always had a key. Just like we always had two sets of pool balls.

Mother never had just one of anything. When she learned how to do something right, she always went into mass production. Let that rattle around in your head. Like those ski hats every grandkid knows how to make. When she started that project, she had to make herself a frame, a circular frame with notched pegs. What she ended up doing was making everyone and their dog ski hats one year, and everyone and their cat ski hat frames the next. And I have been getting knitted ski hats for Christmas ever since. But all that stuff's gone now. I saw some kid carrying the last frame out to the car weeks ago, some kid carrying a hoop around his neck like a winner's wreath.

Jarvis was the oldest unmarried brother that same summer our father had the stroke. He was the old man's arms and legs. "Jarvis get me this. Jarvis get me that." And Jarvis, in the old man's estimation, was the laziest son-of-a-bitch he'd ever had. Out of all his sons. One rotten apple. Jarvis was fifteen, just beginning to grow out of his skin. And I remember the fight they had with the cane.

But who can remember how it started? Over what task or other Jarvis had failed to perform. "What you have to learn is how to take orders. Listen to me when I'm talking to you." I believe those are the universal lines. "Listen to me when I'm talking." And Jarvis never listened. He only talked back. "When you have something important to say, I'll listen." Just a little nine-word sentence like that escalated the war to the nth degree. Just some little syntactical attack did that. And then the old man hit him with his cane, hit him when he had his back turned, so that it came down across his shoulders and back. And Jarvis, quick on his feet, grabbed the cane out of his hands, so that the old man was pulled forward off balance before he let go. Pulled forward so that they almost touched faces before they backed away in surprise.

But then Jarvis broke the cane across his knee. Broke it in the second try and flung the pieces off into the weeds and left the old man to stagger back to the house in his rage. And that's where it didn't stop. That's where Jarvis thought he had won and was finally free of tyranny. But he was wrong.

The first time Jarvis left home, it was really only a trial run. He spent the night in the barn, and everybody thought that he had left for good but me. And I knew where he was because I followed him. When a person turns on their heel like that it always means business. So I followed him first to the neighbors, where he had squeezed himself in between two sheds, into a hollow alley of bull thistles. And I listened to him there, listened to his anger culminate in strategy, listened until another Jarvis voice came through, a voice that wanted to tell stories to his little sister as we both sat on the loose boards in the bull thistles and rocked in pain.

It was a Jarvis voice I had never known, and have not known since. It was a sibling voice almost human. Not like at the funeral when he and his kids ransacked our mother's house. Not like then. But out in the bull thistles, Jarvis sat there sweaty and cold, and told me stories, and I promised I would never tell about how he was going to live in our barn for six years so he could be free. But as it turned out, he only stayed that one night. And the next day they were back at it again, the same old fight without an end.

The next time Jarvis ran away, it would be the real thing. And it would be because of me. Because I wasn't supposed to tell. Only I didn't tell. I would never tell. Only I can't remember exactly how it happened. I just know that when Jarvis lit out like before, I remembered the first time when we sat in the bull thistles telling stories, and I followed him there again, just like before. But this time when I slipped in between the sheds, the old man was right behind me, and the way it came out was, I gave away the whole damn thing. And this was the start of my bad reputation. From that point on I couldn't be trusted.

I couldn't be trusted with any of the family secrets connected with Jarvis. I was just supposed to keep my mouth shut and mind my own business. But I found out about Jarvis moving pipes for Knudtsen. I couldn't help it. I always watched the boys in the fields moving pipe, and one day there was Jarvis. And I caught hell for just finding out. And again the matter was impressed upon my mind. You are never supposed to tell. And what the hell did I ever say about it? What did I ever do? But the old man found out about where Jarvis had run away to, and that's when the old man went after Jarvis with the gun. And that solidified my reputation and was the reason Jarvis had to move to southern Idaho to live with our uncle. That was the reason.

It was a mixed-up mess. Old paint blistered from the sun. I

suspect that it has festered all these years. And was the reason why Jarvis took me down to the ground when he came back after high school, after the old man had died, and Jarvis thought he was the big man of the family then, and rubbed cow dung in my face. It was as good a reason as any.

So most of my brothers and sisters think I grew up with the soft life. Coming along when I did and growing up after the old man died, growing up without brothers and sisters I had to share things with. And they have all hated me for it, for not having had to go through the hard times, the hand-me-downs, the do-withouts. Like because I was the last one to be born, I am somehow not entitled. Like I don't belong. But they have been wrong about that. They are the ones who don't belong. I was an only child out of ten. That's the way it always was. Just me and Mother. And they have their nerve coming here and taking our things, mine and Mother's. These people. These strangers who call themselves my brothers and sisters. They are the ones who are not entitled. They are the ones who moved out.

And they have already taken. All these years since the old man died, they have been coming back to take their share, coming back to borrow tools that never were returned, hammers and wrenches that just walked off. And they have come back for bigger things—all the saddles, all the cans, all the ladders, all the ropes. Everything that didn't belong to a woman, they took. And Mother had to engrave her name onto every screwdriver and wrench to prove that they were ours. And the oldest son complained, "All this should have been mine. I was the oldest son. It all should have come to me." All that male lineage crap. And older sisters, who think I came along too late and didn't have to do any work, didn't have to cook for the crew of brothers, they complain, too. My sisters say that all old things, things that came before, should go to them. The oak dressers, the brass beds, the antiques. It's only right. This is what they say, but none of them are brazen enough to do anything about it. All of my siblings are just too civilized. All of them, that is, except for Jarvis. He grew up somewhere else. He is not even related.

And Jarvis, from the outset, made it clear where he stands. "I don't care what I get. All's I want is my fair share." As if someone was out to gyp him, like he had been cheated his whole life by the rest of us, like we hate him or something because he grew up with our uncle. Jarvis wants his fair share. They all want their fair share. They are all entitled.

My sisters want their fair share because they were here first. And I want my fair share because I was here last. And then there's Jarvis. He wants his fair share for being the old man's arms and legs, for being the one who was made to work against his will. He wants his fair share for the broken cane, and for the gun. There is always the gun, the gun that tips the scales for Jarvis. How much inheritance will it take for us to pay for our father's gun? How much inheritance would it take if you were the one who had to take away the gun from your invalid father, the gun he was pointing at you?

But enough of relatives. I said I would paint the house. I mix the paint in slow. It is almost ready.

So I have discovered that when you make a deal to paint a house, you find things that you didn't expect, things you have to fix before you can get on with your work. You pull back the curtain in the basement shower and find dry rot in the window casing. You run your hand along painted cement, and it chips off where the water has been running down. Or you look at the wall in the hallway where you were supposed to paint a mural, that time when you were taking art classes over at the lake. You were supposed to paint a mountain scene that would remind your mother of the ranch, and of the time when she lived there with the old man. You were supposed to paint a picture of the good times. Paint the fence standing up, even though it had fallen down. And then you remember why it never got done. You remember you couldn't compromise your adolescent integrity, so you put it off until nobody really cared whether you painted it or not.

And because things like that nag at the back of your mind, this is what you do. You find some old cans of paint under the stairs, old cans that are half full from painting the house before. And you've already got new paint, a five-gallon can of beige, to paint the whole inside of the house with. But you remember that your mother always hated beige and white, and all light colors, because it got dirty so fast, so she always painted with darker shades, a darker pink, a darker green, a darker turquoise blue. And you find the cans, and you remember the wall, and you mix the paint, and you remember every piece of junk your brothers and sisters carted off. And then you remember how your father used to yell at the last, "I'm going to have the say in the house. I'm going to have all the say. Listen to me when I'm talking." And you remember that at least one part of him is still you, and this is the way it comes out. You decide to paint the wall. You decide to do it because you were told. And you roll on the paint from top to bottom, bold smooth strokes over the dark pink of the decade before. But this is the difference. You paint it blue. Bold, smooth, turquoise strokes, instead of the beige, because you remember one other thing, what the real estate lady said—that turquoise won't sell.

THE HUNSAKER BLOOD

That spring in 1955, the floor in my parents' bedroom suddenly dropped out, just gave way one day when the old man was walking through, and then there it was, the truth we had all been avoiding—the orange, acrid smell of dry rot.

We had all been sidestepping the issue, the issue of the dry rot and of building the new house. We had known that something was the matter with the floor because of the way it felt when you walked across, like walking on cracked ice. But we didn't like to think about it. And besides, the old man said he needed a new truck, and Mother said, "So that is that." So we had all been waiting, letting things go because someday we were going to build.

And then that spring the floor dropped out when we least expected it, dropped out on our father after he had been ill for so long and we thought that he was getting better.

And that's when I became head nurse, my father's own little Florence Nightingale, the one who would bring him candy pills in the medical kit that came from the grocery. I was the one who would feel his pulse and take his temperature, while he would say cooing things, how's-my-little things, and he would tell me how everyone was against him and try to get me on his side.

So I was on his side, more Sanderson than Hunsaker. And that was a good thing because you didn't want to have anything to do with Hunsakers, if you could help it—one of them Hunsakers who took everything they could lay their hands on. Like the Hunsaker brothers who came to the wedding on foot and left on the old man's best horse. Bloodlines always showed. You could count on that. You could follow it back on your own genealogical chart, two lines traced back to Adam, one through the Sanderson line by way of William the Conqueror and the other through the Hunsakers by way of Attila the Hun.

Mother was a Hunsaker. And the old man would sit there in front of the television in the summer of his growing paralysis, polishing apples, rubbing them on the bib of his overalls, sizing them and knocking off little quips about Attila. Things like "Where's your axe? Where's your horse? Seen any good Hun-sackers lately?"

It was all funny as hell until your mother said, "Just what do you think we are going to live on? Just what do you think we are going to eat?" which suddenly drained all the blood from our veins. Because we knew what that meant, that she had spent the entire winter asking him for money, coaxing last year's logging money out of his savings through the narrow funnel of his pocket, getting it out five dollars at a time.

And he'd say, "Battle axe. Money grabber. This here's money that I earned. And nobody's getting one red cent until they come around." He would say it, and his face would turn red, and he would shake his cane at her for emphasis, and she would walk out the door for $1.25 an hour and leave me home to fetch apples and make scrambled eggs.

68

And that was the big thing back then. Nothing to laugh at. I mean we had spent an entire winter of the old man swinging his cane to get our attention, and then in the spring when we thought that he should be getting better, the floor dropped out, and we were left pushing in cinder blocks and laying down plywood. Because for the first time in five generations of faithful women, our mother had gone to work. Not that she hadn't milked cows and delivered pigs, cleaned house, and fed crews of lumbermen and sons for twenty-five years. But she had never done it for money before, never went outside the boundaries of home, never crossed over that line of his will.

But everyone had to go to work back then. It was the beginning of the end. Everyone with their own assigned job, everyone who was still in the family and wasn't off married or in the marines. And I was the head nurse. My brothers, Harlo watering at the golf course, and Gary setting pins at the bowling alley, and my sister Eileen, recepting for a dentist and trying to save money for dental assistant school. And Mother cleaning houses and bringing home laundry, to the old man's tune of "I'm keeping this money that I have. That's money I've got to retire on. And not one of you is getting a penny until you all stay home where you belong."

And where did we belong really? At the end of his arms? Everyone was beyond arm's length but me, everyone going in their own direction, instead of being there when he needed them. Six sons that had farmed and logged for him, since they were ten and useful, but had been marrying off and leaving home about the time they were just beginning to amount to anything. Until he was down to three, just Harlo and Gary and Jarvis, and then Jarvis running away from home the year before, and now only two left, only two left to take his orders, and there they were beyond his grasp, his failing extremities, the last two to disobey.

And what do you have left with a house that drops out from under you like that, changes on the spur of the moment, makes you hesitate just to put your foot down? What do you have left after the orange, acrid smell, the smell that you get when you lean in close for a hug?

But then, it was money we had all earned, especially the boys who had skipped school to skid logs. But it was money we couldn't touch, money held over our heads. And Mother would say, "We have to go on living. What do you expect us to do?" And she would pave the way for everyone else, open up a hole in the wall of possibility. "This is what all of us have to do," she would say. "We have to go on living."

And everybody was working, only me and the old man at home whiling away our time. Trying to think of things to do to keep ourselves out of mischief, watching "Rin Tin Tin" and "Howdy Doody," and "I Led Three Lives." Switching the channel back and forth, arguing over Clarabell the clown and the guy saving the world from communism. Whiling away our time trying to think up things that would break the monotony—like saddling my horse. And the one day when he tried that, when he went out and threw a blanket and saddle on Old Coalie, and cinched the saddle down tight, he forgot about the bloat, forgot about how a horse that's been cinched up too tight once will remember and bloat up after that when you are cinching. Then when you go to get in the saddle, he relaxes. And the old man forgot about that, forgot and put his foot in the stirrup and started up and the saddle flipped 180 degrees under the horse, and there was my old man upside down under the belly of Old Coalie, hanging on upside down for a split second, before he let go and fell on his back. And that was the end of riding, and we went back to polishing apples and saving the world from communism and Howdy Doody.

And then after it had been a long spring, after everyone had been doing their jobs and everyone was getting used to the idea, it suddenly all came back to the floor. Not the bedroom floor this time, but the kitchen. It all came back to the floor just after breakfast, after I'd fixed my best scrambled eggs with bread like the old man liked. And he started in on the floor, after eating the scrambled eggs, walked across the floor toward the living room and discovered the latest evidence, another soft spot getting ready to go. Another place where we had been holding our breath. We had all noticed it except for the old man, and then he discovered it like he was the first one. And he began to play with it with his feet, putting on his full weight and bouncing just a little. It gave you a sick feeling because you knew that if anyone was going to fall through, it would be the old man. Because he was the one who did it before. It gave you that sick feeling because you didn't know how far the dry rot had spread, and you could see that the old man was getting interested.

"This here floor's got to be fixed," he said. "Rotted clean through." And he stepped on it and stepped back. A kind of gingerly step that you hadn't seen for a long time, and then you knew he was remembering something. Remembering how he was the one who used to do the work of ten men. Nobody could keep up with him, sawing timber, driving a team. That was Alton J. Sanderson, they would say, the toughest SOB in the country. It made you proud you had Paul Bunyan blood in your line.

"This here floor's got to be fixed. And who will fix it if I don't?" he said. And that's how it started, the whole mess with the floor that we had to live with for the rest of the summer and through the winter. First the testing of the floor with his foot, and then the old man going outside to crawl under the house to see how bad it really was. That's how it started. When he came back inside he was covered with black dirt and cat hair.

Next came picking at the corners of the worn linoleum, peeling little chunks off like puzzle pieces. And then he got serious and his mind took hold, and he began ripping the linoleum up like it was shelf paper. The pine wood flooring glared white underneath. And when he'd cleared a good spot over where he said it was worst, he went at it with an axe and wrecking bar, splintering away and prying up the good wood, and crushing through the bad until you began to get whiffs of the mildew smell, the sour smells of rotting lumber under your feet, and you breathed in with the rhythm of the old man's axe. "I'm going to fix this floor," he'd say. "I'll be damned if I'm not." And there he was hacking and hacking, and wheezing between swings, the sweat rolling down his face since the pulling up of the first board. And then, all of a sudden, there it was, the underneath of the house, the black, hard soil smelling of cat urine, cat urine smell coming up through the floor into our kitchen.

He hacked a space the size of a rug, then jumped down and started poking around with his bar. And you could see the dry rot in the beams and the splinters, and see how shrunken and lightweight the wood had become. The uneven hole in my mother's kitchen floor looked like a mouth full of cutting teeth. And there the old man was down in this mouth talking about getting a saw to finish the job, when Mother came home. Came home and caught him down in the hole in our kitchen floor.

"What do you have to say for yourself?" she said to the old man like she was saying it to me, said it like it was time for him to go to bed. And then she said to me, "What did you let him do a fool thing like that for?" And that turned the tables on everything. And I felt like hell about it, and the old man felt like hell about it, and for the rest of the summer we walked a wide path around the plywood they laid across the hole, laid across the hole he tore up but couldn't finish. "Don't nobody touch that hole," he would say. "Don't nobody touch that spot I'm working on, or there will be hell to pay." And the rest of us walked carefully around that spot, felt the kitchen move up and down whenever we walked across, but none of us touched that spot. And we all felt the turn of events, the updraft of change, and knew then that the old floor was gone for good.

And then that fall—"You're not going anywhere without my say. Nobody is going anywhere," he said to Eileen when she was leaving for dental assistant school. Said this to her back as she was walking out the door. "Horse thief. Pickpocket. Bitch! You're not getting any of my money. Not one red cent!"

And the smell of cat urine lingers with me still. But the following spring, when it finally came to tearing down the house, after the old man had died, there was much that was left unexplained. The house, in its dismantling, became a maze of boards and lumber squared off in unfamiliar configurations. There were new piles of lumber where formally solid walls had been, boards nailed across dangerous conditions, and prohibited comfortable old places where you used to walk. And even though you couldn't walk there anymore, there were confined spaces opening up—holes in walls, holes in closets where you could stretch yourself right through like a ghost, like Superwoman. The house was a new maze.

And Harlo and Gary worked all summer wrenching away with crowbars, their backs bared to the sun, the dust and chips of the house freckling their skin. And inside on the walls, there were wall drawings, wall games, condemned-wall graffiti. Every day, walking through to inspect the progress taking place on the house, you would see the artwork taking shape— happy faces, angry faces, stick people in crayon. People in a landscape, people in trees, people hanging out of the windows of houses. The place where someone had written, "Don't write on these walls." And then more writing and games, tic-tac-toe, dot-to-dot, and "Follow this line!" You'd walk in the front door and read, "Follow this line," and you were compelled. And you would follow the stupid line around one room and into the next, into closets and through the holes in back, around windows and up stairs, and then behind some door you would follow this line where it ended in some depraved picture of a naked lady.

And a day later, you would come in and there would be another line in some other color, and you would have to follow that too, another line longer and better than the first, that took you into corners of the house that you had never known before, an interesting line that gave you little notes of encouragement, "Watch where we're going now," "Wasn't that fun," and "We're almost there." Notes in strategic places that kept you going, until there at the end you discovered the ineffable, the quintessential four-letter word, that put you in your place.

And still another line on another day, a line that incorporated the previous lines, continued on after the naked lady, joined in with the unspeakable word in crayon. And this third line was a superior and exceptional new line that took you all the way to the wild attic and back, a line that circled the living room twice and went across the ceiling, a line drawn by some invisible long arm. And then finally, when you thought that maybe it would never end, the line led you to the inscribed words under the stairs, the words drawn like a picture of a note stabbed with a bloody dagger to the wall—"Bless this house!"

And here's the thing. You had followed the line expecting some great revelation, some new word about sex, but all you got was a prayer. A prayer that made no sense. It was more disgusting than the naked lady or the four-letter word. And there that stupid line was where you had to look at it day after day until they pulled it apart and burned it in the field. And you've been thinking about that line for a hundred years. But also about the naked lady. And everything else about the old house.

How they tore down the maze, the graffiti walls, the dry rot floors. How they tore down the maze and slowly transformed it into two piles—lumber reusable and lumber to burn. And the lumber to burn was thrown into the field in one pile, one huge pile for a bonfire, a bonfire that burned hot and high, that ignited your clothes halfway to the house, left little circular burn holes that you didn't notice until the next day and realized you could have burst into flames, spontaneous combustion. One huge bonfire that burned your clothes and singed the hair off both your arms.

A bonfire that burned for days after they got it going, a bonfire bigger than any you would ever see again. A bonfire that burned away the walls and floors of where you lived, the dry rot and the putrid smell, while you moved with your mother and your one brother left, Gary, to a two-room shack across the field. A measly little shack heated by the flame of the kitchen stove and the unshared warmth of your three bodies. A shack that was not half the house that your first house had been. A bonfire that burned into a white heat that left, when it was done, gray smoldering ashes and heaps of red bent nails.

And they tore down the first house, your mother out giving orders to your two brothers, (she was in on it, too), and your brothers bashing in the walls with a crowbar. They were all in on it together. You knew it had to go, but for all these years you remembered the way they did it to the house, not taking it apart logically, systematically, as you would to remedy the question of dry rot, to solve the problem of where you would live, but angrily, brazenly, like finally getting their way.

And finally your mother, in on the thick of it, pulling out the cupboards with a wrecking bar, doing things that you never thought were in her. And then that one time, that one time when you were passing through on your way to the woodpile, there she was in her kitchen with the axe, and you couldn't tell why she was doing it, and you couldn't predict where it would all end, but there was your mother swinging an axe at the last of the black hole. You saw her raise the axe, saw it hesitate in midair, saw it fall. Saw the splinters flying up like before with the old man, and again you felt the rhythm of an idea, felt the rhythm of leveling a house with your will, felt the mixed blood vibrating, ready, in your fingertips. You felt the rhythm, and it all became a part of you then, even at six years, especially at six years. And you felt the changed space, felt the pinpricks of heat upon your arms that were slowly burning you away. And even though you couldn't predict where it was all going, you wanted to go along, too. You wanted to take the axe your-self, wanted to swing it high and let it fall.

And all you really remember remembering is the confused state, a maze of confusion that left you burnt and dry and un-knowing. You were miles away from any real knowing. You were so blind you couldn't analyze anything. But there was something that flashed behind your eyes, something in the anticipation of the perpetual question that even your mother would put to you years later, put to you after your sacking some sacred cow, after doing some unspeakable prohibitive thing, put to you by a woman who should have known better than to say to you on the very brink of adolescent discovery, "When are you going to straighten up and fly right?" The perpetual nagging question designed to ruin the rest of your life. But put to you, and here is the nasty taste in my mouth, put to you by the same woman who was forever opening up the space of being and then trying to shut it down, the woman who still lifts the axe high at night in my dreams and lets it fall. A woman like that, who said to her old man, "We have to go on living. What in hell do you think we intend to eat?" A woman with Attila's blood in her veins, our veins, one with the visceral motion of the axe, one with the exposed bloodline, the one exceptional line. A woman like that—with the Hunsaker blood.

RAT REUNION SUMMER

It was a great day when I did not pass out because of the rat. Eileen said, "You stay by that door, and I will go in this door, and chase him out of the closet there." And she pointed at where I was kneeling on the floor in front of the first door with a pie plate in my hand. Then when the rat came through, there was a great scurry of frantic feet past my knees. But the important thing is—I did not run. I did not run, scream, or faint. It was a great day for little sisters, a great day for womankind. For when we finally convinced the rat to run in the right direction, we managed to pin him permanently between the wall and a free-flying utensil drawer.

We did this because rats are a serious matter. It is important to remember that. In the clinches. You never want to turn your back on an overconfident rat. He moves when you move. Takes

up the slack in the distance between you. You turn around and
there he is three feet closer. Nearer the mark. So you have to
face him off. Nose to nose. It's the only way.

Denton and I have lain awake for a week in the loft of our
unfinished cabin in the mountains of northern Idaho, listening
for another rat. There is only this one rat. We are pretty sure.
Only one who came in through a hole in the eaves when we
piled some boards against the outside, only one we heard
squeaking his twigs in between the wall and the tin roof and
saw disappear in our flashlight beam, cat-like into the wall.

Every night we listen for the sounds of rustling, the slight
cough of something disturbed. We know he is still there, although we haven't seen him for two days. We know he is still
there because every morning we find the black nuggets of his
indiscretion, placed in patterns of three all over the cabin floor,
by the woodbox, by the door, beside our shoes and socks.
Little notes he leaves for us, "Kilroy Was Here," "Yankee Go
Home," and "I have not yet begun to fight." Little MacArthur
messages, nibbled in the ends of bread sacks promising, "I shall
return."

And here is the thing. We personify the rat. I know we personify the rat. What else can we do when he scratches rat tracks
across our dreams? We have to play his game. We have to play
by his rules. We have to stay on the same rat wavelength, or we
may miss everything.

I fold back the covers for a minute. I think I heard something. I listen in the night air, my face suddenly cold. "Do you
hear anything?" I whisper. Denny comes out for air, too, tunes
in his radar in the direction of the rail. "Sounds like the kitchen."

"Are you sure? Are you sure it wasn't by the door?" We have
left the poison by the door.

"No, the kitchen sink. I think he is thirsty."

We hear nothing for awhile, get cold, and then cover our
heads again. This is the way we sleep. We leave as little as possible to chance. We pull in our arms and legs, never leave them
dangling out over the side to attract things that go bump in the

night, never leave an excess of anything exposed, an invitation to rat bite. There is only the tiny opening for our faces in the covers, only our senses sticking out, for breathing and for listening. There is no such thing as an absolutely quiet rat.

And this has been our camping experience this summer, getting ready for the family reunion, putting in windows, putting in doors, putting in the loft, putting in rat-protection. Eileen says, "I don't know how you can stand to sleep out there with a rat," a comment aimed at only the four-legged kind. Eileen is safe and secure over at the old house, safe and asleep within the same walls where we killed the closet rat, the closet rat that Eileen said was smaller than the both of us. "I don't know how you can sleep with a rat," my sister says, the same sister that only yesterday stood safe across the room, saying "Get him, Franki. Get him," as we chased some incredibly small field mouse across that same kitchen, only out the back door this time.

And she is the one who put me up to this, twenty-five years ago, the one who said I was brave to stand up to the first rat, the one who made me afraid to admit that I was afraid. Eileen, my sister, whose feet have turned to clay after all these years.

So this is her fault. I owe it all to her. My face will be gnawed away before I will admit that I am a coward. As for Denny, there is nothing in particular that he has to prove, but he will stay here by my side, spending a faithful rat-vigilance in the loft of our cabin.

We listen for the sounds of rolling dice, rat games on the lower level. Denny thinks he hears something. I think about the poison we have put out, the boxes of pellets placed where the rat would least expect it. Little red boxes of insecurity that will drive him wild for water, will drive him out the door we have left slightly ajar on his behalf. It is much more subtle than a gun. The only problem is, if you leave the door open for the rat to go out, there is no telling what else might come in. It is one of the great rat dilemmas, like all things in life.

At the entrance to the property, the family property, we have installed a gate, a great green farmer's gate chained between a great tree and a cement post. Judd installed the gate, Judd, the brother with the most to lose because of his investment in his cabin. So far we have a community of three—the old house that has been Eileen's since Mother died, the barn that Judd turned into his cabin and started this whole reunion business by making this a nice place to come to, and the woodshed, which is where we are lying in our unfinished state, listening for the rat.

So we installed the gate in early spring. We've been here on and off all summer. In July we had the reunion. And through it all has been the irritating presence of Jarvis. Jarvis, the youngest next to me, Jarvis who has an unnerving way about him. Who comes up here with nothing much to do and gets annoyed because we won't stop our work and talk to him. Who keeps coming by to borrow things, things we hauled seven hundred miles to use ourselves on our cabin.

Jarvis, of course, was offended by the gate. "Who do you think you are locking out?" he says. "Why didn't anyone tell me about the gate?" Jarvis came when nobody was expecting him. Came three days early to the reunion, while Denny and I were in town getting supplies. Came pulling his pickup and camper with a Volkswagen.

There are two stories about the camper and the Volkswagen. The first one goes like this: "Halfway over the pass, the pickup threw a rod, and we had to come on the rest of the way pulling it with the Vee-Dub." This is Jarvis's story. But Jarvis has many kids. And the way they tell it, when you have one of them off in the corner, pumping her for information, is this: "We pulled the camper all the way from Washington. Daddy wanted something to stake his claim with." That is, Jarvis towed this trash-heap of a pickup camper all the way from Washington state because he wanted to dump it on family land, wanted to ditch his trash in the valley of our rustic retreat, an eyesore for the deer to graze around, oxidized aluminum in the periphery of our zoom lens. And that's my brother Jarvis, grinding the gears of his Volkswagen, just so that we would all remember that he too is entitled.

And what do you do with a brother like that? Who thinks you are out to gyp him? Who measures everyone else by the standards he sets for himself? Who comes up here packing a bolt cutter to insure his rights.

The deal with the chain has been going back and forth. It may never end. Judd put up the chain with the intention of keeping out the "uninvited." And Jarvis saw through that, thought the chain was made just for him. To keep him off the family land. Judd made a big stink about giving him a key, then didn't, so Jarvis comes up here unannounced and clips his way through with the bolt cutters. Then he puts on his own cheap lock in the place of a missing link, put some ornery cheap thing in between as a link, some cheap lock it only took Judd one try to smash off. And now Judd says that Jarvis is not getting a key even if he does ask nice. But Jarvis will come through. I'm putting my money on Jarvis.

So it has been a big summer for attracting relatives. The cool weather and no mosquitoes drew them, the smog-free air and potato salad lunch, the open land and cracker pie, the old home place drew them, drew them like flies to the family reunion. In bigger numbers than ever before, in bigger campers, bigger tents, bigger families. Bigger plans for building their own cabins up here. We've tried to get out the word that it's already crowded enough. But still they come to the reunion with all their plans, waving their arms in the direction of imaginary structures, and all their four-wheelers stirring up the dust. Let's not forget about that. And all their talking around our campfire, into all hours of the night. All their teenagers sneaking in and out of the brush, darting adolescent eyes at one another across our conversation. And then there has been Jarvis and his gun.

Someone should write and tell these people that a dog is not the same thing as a kid. We have to put up with their kids, but we do not have to put up with their dogs. And dogs that are on their last legs, we especially could do without them. They are not at all inclined to be friendly, even if we are related. Such a dog does not know the difference between a first cousin and a second, once or twice removed. We are all the same to him under the skin, all alien, and he sits guarding the porch, no respecter of persons, baring his teeth like he wants to take off your leg. Someone should write and tell these people. So Jarvis doesn't have to.

Here's the scenario. Here is cousin Wallace, young cousin Wallace coming to the reunion for the first time, for the first time since he's been off drugs, bringing his dog, the only living being he truly loves in the whole world, bringing this dog to play frisbee with in the field. And get this. Wallace keeps a journal on the dog, keeps a journal on the best frisbee-playing dog in the world, a record of the number of frisbees thrown, and the number of frisbees caught. Writes it all down in his frisbee book, about the dog with the ninety percent average. And another thing, the dog has cancer. He is not expected to live to the end of the year. And still one more thing, the dog especially likes to nip at Jarvis's kids. Nips at them without warning when one of them wants something obnoxious like to come in the house. (And who said dogs lack intelligence?) Jarvis gets upset at this, his little muffins being mauled by Wallace's dog. So this is what Jarvis does. Good old Jarvis. He walks up to Wallace when he's petting Buzzy—the dog's name is Buzzy—he comes up to Wallace and pulls a pearl-handled derringer out of his pocket and says, "You do something about that dog, or I will." A kind of family-reunion-make-my-day.

Good old Jarvis. About as much tact as a cement truck. I think we can predict that this will be the last we see of Wallace, as well as Buzzy.

But Jarvis will still be around. He is made of sterner stuff. You couldn't knock him down with a crowbar. Or dissuade him from showing up at the reunion, not when real estate is involved. Jarvis went to real estate school. He knows the value of land. Right at first, we all thought that going to real estate school was going to help, the lessons they give on how to attract potential buyers, the personality improvement part. We all thought it was going to help. He was nice for an awful long time. Then he went into remission. Went back to his normal self and became the old Jarvis that we all "know and love," the good old Jarvis who comes to the reunion with a chip on his shoulder.

Jarvis, who is trying to push his weight around. This is what we say about him. He is the punchline of all our jokes. We say, "Who ate the cookies?—Jarvis." "Whose spare tire shall we roll down the hill this year?—Jarvis's." "What's the difference between an elephant and a breadbox?—Jarvis." We pelt him with all of our verbal abuse, and still he keeps coming back for more. A little slower every year, less quick with his response, which makes us think we are wearing him down.

Of course, there are other subjects that one can bring up around Jarvis which are especially rewarding. One of them is women's rights, or women's lib, which is the term that he would recognize. So Jarvis comes over to our cabin to borrow a screwdriver, and five or six two-by-fours to lay across his camper while he is repairing a leak. "Look's like *she* cleaned up around here since I was here before," (my emphasis added). I notice this while I'm painting around a window. "What do you mean *she*?" I say. "Denny did that while I was fixing the saw, the skillsaw, which coincidentally was invented by a woman." I sprinkle this information out like I am chumming fish.

"Should have known. Should have known," he says, and takes a handful of nails. He takes a handful of nails because he is building a porch for his camper, a porch out of our two-by-fours.

Jarvis is good at playing this game. It intimidates the living rat bait out of me. Makes me wonder what will still be here when I come back some time. What will be left after Jarvis comes up when we're not here and makes his rounds. Jarvis and his sticky fingers.

I say to Jarvis. "What is it exactly that you plan to do with your lot? Are you going to start a cabin this year?" Jarvis doesn't answer immediately. There is something grinding away underneath.

"One of these days," he says.

When we talk about cabin building, it is coming close to the mark. Close to the poison by the door. Judd and Eileen are the trustees for this place. They have the final say. Big brother and big sister having the final say. It rubs Jarvis raw.

"It takes more planning, more figuring, when you have to do it from scratch," he says. And then he adds, almost as an afterthought, "You had it easy."

We had it easy, me and Denny, traveling seven hundred miles just to put in a nail, seven hundred miles for two or three weeks out of the year, seven hundred miles for the last three years and still we have not replaced the roof, the roof of the old wood-shed we have slowly been turning into our cabin. The galva-nized steel roof that Jarvis and everyone else shot to pieces when they were boys. The roof that leaks like a sieve if we don't patch it every time we're here.

"Sure, Jarvis, everyone's got it easy," I say. "This place wouldn't be here if it hadn't been for Judd. The way I figure is that he has a right to have the say. And he does have the legal say."

This gets him where he lives. He looks off in the distance. "So you are in with them," he says.

"I'm not in with anybody. That's just the way it is." And then Jarvis begins to stretch himself, begins to flex the self-assurance that I thought was wearing down. He has one ace in the hole. He always does.

"You and Eileen got that title yet?" he says, and the corners of his mouth begin to curl. And this is the ultimate weapon in the war we have been waging. Jarvis's ultimate threat. The last time this place was surveyed was shortly after Lewis and Clark.

And the survey markers are old and the survey markers are gone, but Jarvis finds them. He has taught himself "surveyoring," just so that he can come up here to measure the land with his used equipment. Climbs all over the hills in front of the house with it, climbs all over the hills in back. Spends one whole reunion surveying our land. The land our mother left to us, the whole family, in trust. The land that none of us will be able to sell until it is surveyed.

His surveying makes everyone nervous. "What are you trying to prove, Jarvis? Just what are you trying to prove?" "I'm not trying to prove anything," Jarvis says. "Just don't want to build a cabin on a piece of property unless it is mine. Just don't want to take a chance on losing it."

And here is the rub. The results of Jarvis's survey, the hold he has over all of us. Back when the place was sold, back when it was sold and resold and traded around in the family, and then sold back to the government, all but these ten acres, someone made a great mistake, some county engineer who wrote the coordinates on the title, who squared off our land from someone else's memory. Someone made a great mistake and said our property is here, when it was really supposed to be over there. They wrote it down and changed the way it had been for a hundred years. Put us down over there, thirty yards on the other side of the house, the house that has always been in this family, but is really a figment of our imagination.

And this is where he gets us, makes us all pull the covers up over our heads. "You all can go along building your pipe dreams," he says. "But just in case the Forest Service gets any notions, I'm building over there." He waves his arm in the direction of the house, indicating the other side. "And when I record the title, I will have to record it right. And that will leave you all sitting out here in thin air. I will record my cabin as being on the edge of the land, and that won't leave you on the edge of anything, because you are really on government land. I have to do it," he says. "I'm conscience bound."

And that's my brother Jarvis, squeaking his twigs in between the roof and the wall and setting all our nerves on edge. Nerves that didn't have to be set on edge. For as far as we have been concerned all these years, what the government doesn't know won't hurt them. As far as the Forest Service is concerned, this is our place, our place unless anyone goes messing around with a survey and fiddling with county records. Eileen has put it this way, "If he thinks he's going to get a title out of me, it will be over my dead body." She says. And that is the end of that story.

So there have been more than a few rats at this reunion, as Denny and I have pounded our few nails into the hollow shell of the cabin. It has been a rat reunion summer, in fact, with us lying awake nights listening to the gnawing going on beneath us, under our loft, the loft we have built out of pipe dreams. A pipe dream. Some drug-induced hallucination, I suppose. I've never really thought about it before—some metaphor that has lost its meaning, but has come scratching its way back between the cracks of a new idea. It all makes perfect sense now, now that I've seen up close the beady eyes of the rat—the cabin rat standing on confident tiptoe, blinking his pink eyes and waggling his rope tail—the mountain cabin rat who pokes his head out for just a peek from the insulation tear, before burrowing deep and safe inside our cabin walls.

CAT ISLAND

Melody O'Mally lived in the smallest house in Hayden Village. It was a cracker-box, a matchbox, a place to stick your grasshoppers. It was the smallest house under the tallest trees, sitting back from the road on a long rutted horseshoe drive that half circled a desert of dry weeds. Dry weeds, in spite of the perpetual attempt of one twirley-bird sprinkler that made half-hearted figure eights in the air.

That was Melody O'Mally's place, a dried scab to look at when riding past the golf course on the way to the lake. But that wasn't Melody O'Mally, her bed still pulled out at midday from the guts of the sofa, beer cans lining the wall like targets, her father's underwear strapped across the chair beside her. Not in the summer after eighth grade graduation, that one long summer before bussing into town for the tail end of junior high, ninth grade. The junior high where they locked everyone out in the rain until the ten-minute bell and taught us all what it meant to be less than human. The junior high where Melody O'Mally finally came out of her shell and filled our shared locker with brown paper novels and thought it was funny as hell how the science student teacher showed the ninth grade boys how to pick locks. So that when we went to put away our algebra, some subhuman, with the flick of his wrist, would pop open our lock and hand it to us gratis, and we were only surprised when we opened the door and didn't find something even more gratuitous hanging from the middle hook.

Later I would discover the changed chemistry of junior high—the crowd huddled across the street around the stop sign, intense faces smoking madly, familiar faces doing strange new things. It was like picking up a rock and finding the worms that had always been there. Little worms, little surprises at myself for wanting to shut Ronda Sue Patterson up about Melody, while at the same time wishing I could tell Melody to get her junk the hell out of our locker. And there I was discovering these things, poised on the brink of some clarifying statement.

But the summer before, when the lake was still a paradise of white caps, there was no need for clarification. No need for Ronda Sue Patterson's voice of victory, morality, and chaos, to try and explain it to us. That summer when Melody O'Mally emerged from the stale air and the crumpled heaps of living in her cracker-box, she shed the walls of her place like shedding old skin—and she was iridescent.

As if she'd had, in that long summer second, an environmental bypass. A reprieve from the twirley-bird sprinkler wetting the same brown spot every week like the only place a cow can lick her own rump. A reprieve to a higher shade of green. For Melody lived on the road that demarcated in grass tones the difference between the resort people and the rest of us. People like me who lived on an open hill, surrounded by timothy and all the agricultural microbial things that got in one's clothes and got in one's hair and distinguished one in a petri dish. For whatever divine reason, Melody had been born apart from all of that. And that summer she moved even further up the scale of summer greens by which we all measured ourselves and came out knowing the people of whom the rest of us had only dreamed.

A person could have cried over the people she knew. She knew Sydney with a "y," who knew how to ballet. And she knew Donna who knew Bing, at his summer home. And she knew Ferrol who knew that she knew that he owned his own boat, an inboard-outboard. And she knew a rodeo queen with a silver crown. And she knew these people by name and by code and said their names as easily as pulling on an oar. And she spoke of them often but not with spite, as you would to make a listener feel like dirt, but with respect, like a ritual. "Hello, Miami. Hello, Texas. I'm thinking of you." A ritual that drew in their various lives, from wherever they lived the rest of the year, and brought us all that much closer to the Emerald City.

And there we were that summer, saying these names in whispers as we talked above the lazy pulse of sprinklers on the golf course greens. Talking until dawn about Bing Crosby's bathtub filled with beer, the location of Marilyn Monroe's mole in relationship to the North Star, and other assorted theories of continental drift. Or we rode our horses down Lover's Lane in the day, me riding our buckskin, Duke, and Melody sitting astride our finest palomino mare, Golden Dream, both of us riding silent through the forest, letting the dark woods speak to each of us in its own way.

And riding horses was almost as fine as lying under the stars. And lying under the stars was almost as fine as owning a boat. And so it was finally arranged that Melody should get us a boat from the place where her father worked, in order to complete the tapestry of the universe. The one that had us sun-

89

ning ourselves on a catamaran, or skimming across the bay in a sloop to Bing's Point, or even rowing by hand a dull green dinghy across the chopping waves. We needed at least that much. And got it, as fine as any green dinghy around. For it was being on the water that mattered, the sea, as opposed to viewing the white-capped waves from the houses that we cleaned. It was the water itself, with Melody there, sunning herself as I rowed, her long strawberry hair curling bashful around her chin.

And Melody saying, "I will row. I will take my turn." And me nodding her away from the oars, thinking how could I let her row? How could I allow it? When the plan had already gotten ahead of itself in my mind, the plan of me rowing her across to Bing's Point, where we would disembark and eat our sandwiches in the star-studded shade. So I rowed, but things turned out differently than planned. For when we got across the bay, the water was too deep to get to shore and the submerged rocks too problematic to land. So we set ourselves back to the open sea and the spray and the wake of the summer speedsters, and we called vulgar sailor names at their backs, made vulgar sailor gestures as the water skiers flew by, and at the top of our lungs when we thought that *anyone* could hear, we sang, "My father was the keeper of the Eddystone light. / He married a mermaid one fine night. / And from this union there came three, / a porpoise and a porgy and the other was me."

And I rowed. And the sun beat down on my brains, burning across the part in my hair, but on Melody coating her with mother-of-pearl, her arms and legs cocoa-buttered, her fingers and toes painted in coral shades. When she moved, she left sliding streaks of oil upon the bench.

"In the spring, when the water turns," she said, "you knew the water turned, didn't you? Well it turns. All the water from the bottom, the cold water, comes up to the top, and all the water on the top sinks down to the bottom. The water turns over. In the spring when the water turns, it brings all this polluted water up to the top and that's why we have to boil the drinking water in the spring, just a few weeks every April. You knew that, didn't you? Of course. Well, one year when the water turned, it brought up this dead man who had been down on the bottom. He had been down there for over a year. He was all white and puffy. They never did find out who he was. But the lake is like that."

"I didn't know," I said.

"Yes. They say that there are underground rivers. There was this man who jumped off Tubb's Hill and drowned himself in Coeur d'Alene Lake, and they found him out at Hayden. That's happened several times. I'm surprised you hadn't heard," she said, pulling out a bottle of orange soda from beneath the bench, an opener from her beach bag.

"Care for a pop?" she said. And me, pulling on the oars, licking the dried dumb corners of my mouth and rubbing them dry again with my fingers, I listened. Who could talk about continental drift out there? Who could say anything, but Melody?

"When the lake freezes over, have you ever seen the lake freeze over? When the lake freezes over people have been known to drive their cars across it. That's how Elmer Hunt drove his jeep through the ice. You remember about Elmer Hunt. He thought he would be smart and drive his jeep across the bay, but summer people don't know much about winter up here, always off living somewhere in the sun. Except for the Hunts because they lost all their money, so they stay year round. All that money she won on the quiz show and their insurance. So Elmer Hunt drove his jeep through the ice and had to hire some frogmen to go down and get it. I bet it was cold. Pass the chips."

Melody in her sunglasses, lifting her lips to the sun, dared them to burn. She took the chips.

"Their kid is funny anyway. They don't go to parties much. Everybody talks about the Hunts. Very strange people. She has the gardener into lunch. Get it? Into lunch. That old man. Green jeans and all. There is a story to tell about that, you can bet."

"Where shall we go now?" I said.

"Ever been to Cat Island?" she said, a chip poised between two fingers. "I been there once. I camped overnight. They call it Cat Island because years ago some old trapper came out of the mountains with a lot of gold, and he came back to town to marry his sweetheart, only she had packed up and left with no forwarding address, only leaving a passel of cats. And the old trapper gathered all those cats and kittens of hers and carried them off to Cat Island. Only it wasn't Cat Island yet, not until all those cats had had kittens and their kittens kittens, and there were hundreds of cats all over the place, all of them keeping the old man company and reminding him of his lost love, but keeping him busy catching fish to feed all those hungry mouths, mouths that would as soon be gnawing on a fish bone as look at you. But they were mouths he felt duty-bound to feed until his dying day, and one day he did die. And when they found him, the old trapper, he had been picked clean down to the bone. And they never did find the gold.

"And you didn't know about Cat Island? You can't see it's an island from here or from the shore. You have to go around it in a boat. It's over there."

I stopped rowing and looked behind me. The island. There it was. The beginning of an idea. I will row Melody to Cat Island, my left brain said. I will row her there, where she has been before. I will row her all the way to Cat Island and that will be something. And just as I turned, Melody brushed with both hands the crumbs away from her breasts. "Very messy," she said, pulling her halter top out, coaxing with one finger the last of the stubborn crumbs.

So the thing about Melody is this. She had always been there. When I take out my picture of first grade, there she is in the front row dressed in some washed-out blue clothes, smiling some washed-out blue smile, some sick grin between two ears. Melody O'Mally in the slow readers, Finches they called themselves. We were the Hawks, and we could read Dick and Jane faster than anybody. I do not remember Melody too well in first grade except for that. Nor in the second. But she had always been there, through Schneberger, through Parks, through Gordon. Our little first grade enclave working itself up through the ranks, never running in the halls, never fighting on the playground, always honor class, standing in front of the honor class banner. We were so good.

But not good enough to notice that there was never any Melody out playing Steal the Flag, marbles, or Hole-in-the-Bucket. All those playground games that were our real curriculum. No Melody making pine needle houses under the trees in first grade or sliding into first base in fifth. No Melody at all until eighth grade, and then there she was, all of a sudden, growing her hair long while everybody else was giving book reports. She was the first one. And to me, it made what we did to her in PE, always picking her last to be on the team, seem so shabby. How could I forgive myself? But by then she didn't really seem to care about playing ball. So perhaps there was no real harm done. But that made everything all the more difficult, because I couldn't get to know her by letting her use my mitt. And I couldn't talk the boys into letting her bat first. It was all so very depressing. All I could do was help her with her math and pass notes back and forth to her in study hall about how silly we thought everyone else was.

And then in the summer after eighth grade graduation, when I rode my bike down the horseshoe drive to her house and went flip-flip over the hose, and I met at last her mother and father, and I found out they drank and they fought all the time, I loved her all the more. And she was mine. Melody was all mine, I had discovered her. And I had discovered her before the boys, before the rush. And that was something.

That summer in the boat with Melody was supreme. Her pink lips, slightly orange from the soda, rehearsing the legends that had been her primer.

"Gary Crosby paid Donna's father five dollars for a tuna fish sandwich." Donna went to parochial school, and the only one who knew her was Melody.

But the more I rowed, the further away the island seemed.

And it became an obsession, a fantastic idea. I must get Melody to the island where she had been before. I must get her back to that point, let her lie out on the beach and finish her tan. I must suspend every other idea, hold every aching muscle in check. I did not care so much for my own tan, a tan that would always be "a working tan." But Melody had a real tan, a leisure tan. It was worth rowing for.

In ninth grade history the teacher, Mr. Barrett, would say, "There are only two kinds of women in this world. Those who do, and those who don't." He gave simplified multiple-match tests, the kind where once you've used the A or the B you never have to worry about them again. You just match one column with the other, spend ten minutes before the test matching the columns of former tests to get an A. But even at this, there were only a few of us pulling straight As, only a few of us who could see through his simplicity. And yet when he said that there were only two kinds of women in this world, we all believed him.

Melody and I never did reach the shore of Cat Island. Never lay shipwrecked out on the sand, never crawled half dead, half alive like Quentin Reynold's *20,000 to One*. Never went skinny-dipping in the shallow pool that must have waited on the far side, never laughed and giggled at our nakedness. Never struggled in the environment of our language to describe who we really were.

This is Melody, removing her clothes beside the silent pool, swinging her hips and her arms to the motion of an imagined song, trotting in rhythm to the water's edge. And this is Melody, her breast cutting the foam like white caps. And that was me then, but without words, not having to struggle with the abyss that is our language, the dried scab of syntax. Not reducing myself to the used words that describe women, junior high words inscribed on lavatory walls. This is Melody shaking her ass toward the water's edge, shoving her new little tits in your face like the girls in gym class.

Some broad. Is that what I would have called her? Some bitch? Some whore? For I surely knew at the time that there were only two kinds of women, those who knew Ferrol with the boat or Sydney with a "y," and those who lived in the middle of a field of timothy. Did it take a junior high history teacher to show me the demarcations of words? And this is the name of that tune, Melody O'Mally dropping her drawers and shaking her ass toward the sea.

What would I have said, if I had been forced to struggle with saying it then, if we had gone all the way to Cat Island and gone skinny-dipping in the shallow pool, if I had listened to the beckoning calls of the siren of the sea? What would I have said? "Melody slid off her clothes and dropped them defiantly, flinging her hair back, her feet pawing the sand, her hip muscles flexing wildly."

What could I have said with my limited vocabulary? "She was afraid to come out of the water. / She was afraid that the people would see." Would I have said that about Melody? Would I have seen her in that way? Like the way I see her now, the sun waffling down through the trees, as we would have tarried until losing the sun over the basalt of Cat Island, Melody holding my arm as we went under, seeing who could hold their breath, who could open their eyes, who could swim between the legs and not come up being ridden like a horse.

That summer, if we had reached the island, I might have felt the touch of woman's flesh, not the touch of years later when my husband would wrap his hard legs around me in bed, but the touch of soft woman's flesh that holds tight in some embrace and races backward in time toward a mother, some embrace that might have made me ask who we both were, who any of us are—female. Who was this woman, not my mother? Who was this woman, not myself? And that fall when I saw the betrayal, hands reaching around the necks of pimpled faces, saw her kissing at the end of the hall at the end of the day, would I have known anything different? Would I have gone through the cultural evolution of knowing—girl, virgin, temptress, whore?

She was so close. Sitting on the bench in the middle of our boat, close like putting your face up to the neck of a horse, your cheek and ear one with the motion. She was Melody. Just Melody. And I couldn't put my finger on the right words, like I could put my hand on her arm when she stepped into the boat. And I couldn't think of how I was thinking about it. And I didn't want to. I just wanted to let the waves lap against the bow behind me while I rowed, and let Melody droop her golden arm over the side, if she wanted, and trail her finger in the water. And I just wanted everything to stay that way forever. Was that so much to ask?

But then Melody, in that fall when her tan had faded, became porcelain-skinned, a fair madonna. And in the tenth grade, she ran away to Maui to live in a commune. And suddenly my guts ached, like the inside of her couch, the guts of her sofa spread out across the living room, ripped out, lain upon. So that I felt the turn of her body, every curve, every pressure. And I knew then that something had flowered and passed away beyond my grasp. And all I had left was the consolation in my hands, the place along my palms where blisters had formed, and the memory of rowing for my life in one incredible mist of words. The certain memory that it was our body that went to Cat Island, our body without words on a sea of words, drifting on an infinite rhythmic sea, our illusive body sitting on a column of basalt above the shallow pool, telling our tales to the thin air and spreading our lengths with cocoa butter.

WOMAN TALKING
TO A COW

I had to leave Judd and Eileen in the house to come out and carry hay. I had to leave them alone and come out. I know you don't mean anything by it because you got to eat, too, everybody does. But I'm just saying. Everybody's got to eat.

And then there's this here manure fork. See it? Only three tines. You think you got problems. See that? See how it takes me so long? Hay falls right through. Don't blame me all the leaves knocked off by the time I get here. It's not my idea of how to do things. And you can just keep your green tongue to yourself.

No, it's not my idea. What we need is a barley fork. But can we have a barley fork? No-o-o-o. We ain't good enough. I said to him, "Alton, when we getting back our barley fork? Ain't we got as much use for it as Harmon and Clive?" And do you think he'd listen? Do you think he'd stand still for me going over there and getting it, when we could use it right here? His head holds onto an idea about as good as this here fork.

Now watch this. See, what did I tell you? But that ain't the half of it. After this I gotta feed those sheep. "Feed my sheep," he says just like that, and walks out the door like he was Christ himself. Going into town to make some miracle happen, he is. And Judd and Eileen in the house while I'm out here.

That Eileen better mind what she's doing, is all I can say, or I'll blister her good. She can get into more trouble, likes to throw the dishes out of my cupboards, my best dishes, Grandma's flur-de-lees. She climbs up the front like it was a ladder. Throws them down to show Judd. I could beat her brains out. And Judd just one year old, getting the biggest kick out of that. My best dishes with the gold leaf. She's a climber, all right. Boy, can she climb. But I'll blister her good if she does it again. And I will too. I got to do it. She has got to learn.

Don't you maw me. I'm doing the best I can. All you gotta do is stand there. I have to keep after her. She's always into something. Like throwing my pictures into the fire. My pictures of down home. Negatives and all. And there them two were sitting in front of the stove watching them pop and crackle. Little shits. I could have skinned her alive for that one. She always goes for exactly what you don't want her into. She was old enough to know better, too. I wanted to skin her alive.

You think you're standing in the mud. You don't know much about Karakul sheep, do you? Them are those black curly sheep over there. Each one worth about ten of you. That's 'cause they're special. No everyday sheep for us. No sir. We couldn't put our farm money into anything like potatoes or sugar beets. He doesn't listen to me. No, we had to get Karakul sheep. Going to make a killing with those sheep. We made a killing, all right.

Here chew on this. First he gets this special deal on a herd of fifteen sheep. He puts every cent we got into them. I feed them right here one whole winter. Come spring he finds out something. You know what he finds out? The wool on his sheep ain't no good because they're mixed breed. And to make any money you have to have pure breed. And we got fifteen sheep of Karakul and something else. But does he give up on the Karakul sheep business? You can bet your cow cud he doesn't. No. He trades those fifteen sheep down to six. Those right over there. And he called that a deal. Traded the whole herd for six. But they were purebreds. And I was just a woman and couldn't understand a deal like that, now could I?

Now come spring again, he finds out this: each one of them sheep eats two ton of hay a day for the entire winter, and we can't sell that wool. That's right. Do you want to know why? We can't sell it because Karakul sheep don't shear like regular sheep. No. To make them curly black coats for all them women back East, those hundreds and thousands of women dying to buy our wool, you gotta get the wool off of the lambs. That's the finest quality, the fine black wool before it gets coarse. That's what you gotta do. Take it off the babies. And that's what he finds out come spring. And he gives me this here manure fork with only three tines. Move your damned head.

You don't seem to understand, do you? They make those women's coats out of their black curly hides. You gotta skin them to get it. And Alton, he don't find that out until he's got all the money spent. They don't want the grown-up coarse wool. They got to skin the lambs. Peel off them hides no bigger than puppies.

But this is the last thing he finds out. Neither one of us has got the stomach for it. Killing the babies. So we got those six sheep over there eating us out of house and home, and we got a fistful of black curly hides drying hard in the barn, and we got two kids in the house breaking everything I got and waiting to be fed, and we haven't got enough of those black curly hides to make one coat.

And he goes off like that to crack one more deal. Listen here, old gal. You got your nerve to lick my leg and want more hay. You're the last thing on this farm that's worth a damn, so you just better look out.

GRAFFITI
ON THE ROCKS

Sometimes the way I talk is criminal, but that's the way I am. They can't take the country out, if you know what I mean. Besides they can't shoot a woman for what she says in a bar on this planet. Not the last I heard.

Anyway, back to where we were before that last round. About the graffiti of life in the twentieth century. Ever hear this one?

"Old golfers never die—they just lose their balls." Those were the words baked in clay on the plaque on the wall of the place where my mother and I worked when I was young. They were words to live by, like "Walk a mile in my shoes," or "He ain't heavy, he's my brother." They were real words, true words, words you could count on. Words that knocked around in your head for awhile. Like, "Old golfers never die, old golfers never die—they just play through." Or "Old golfers never die—they just break par." And even though the variations weren't as good as the originals, which my mother had to explain to me and then wished she hadn't and had to keep brushing me away from in front of that plaque where I was forever dusting, they were still solid words. Words that rang true. And if you said them just right, to the right person, they were words good enough. Not trendy. Not like the words above some bar and grill—"This ain't Burger King. You'll have it OUR WAY or you won't get the son-of-a-bitch."

You want to pass the pretzels? They weren't like that. Words you will have to explain some day to the first slob that sits up next to you and asks you why that's funny, someone who has never seen the television commercial. No. Those were universal words. Words that hinged in the middle, with truth in the bend of their own irony. They were the old some-things-never-die words—old memories, old sailors, old stogies, who only fade or smell that way. And everybody seemed to understand such brevity back then. Life on a bumper sticker. Graffiti on the rocks. It was always "Jesus Saves," first, before it became "Jesus Saves—Green Stamps!"

I said to her, "Mother," I said. "Why do you want to marry an old duffer like that?" And she kept on dusting there where she was, dusting between the ears of some old iron Siamese cat on the edge of the fireplace grate. I said to her, "Mother, don't you feel just a little bit silly, a woman at your age?" Said it like it was spray painted on rocks.

"What a cliché!" I could have been saying, being sixteen and very much aware of the redundancy of adults. "What a cliché!" I think I did say, but not in so many words.

So where was I when they passed out brains? Sitting somewhere in darkness? In the head-echoing noise of adolescence?

So I said to her, "A wig? Really, Mother. It all depends on *whom* you are trying to impress."

And I can't believe I said that. I have found we say a lot of stupid things when we are young, things only partially and abruptly uttered, that eventually come dragging back like the Ghost of Christmas Past. It all settles in on you some night, while you are trying to digest beer and pizza, parks itself at the end of your kitchenette and recalls for you the time before, when you had gotten yourself to be so damned smart.

Anyway, in the spring Mother and I would open the Conway house. She would take the brass key from her ashtray in the blue Chevy, untangle the knotted leather chain from the maze of other keys, and we would walk down the lane, carrying our cleaning rags and disinfectants under our arms, through the dark trees to the Conway house.

And if we were lucky, when we opened the door, it would only smell like moth balls. Dead little surprises in the sink did not impress us, dehydrated mice that had come in with a terrible thirst, or squirrels that had scratched themselves down the chimney uninvited. We could have lived without the cliché of nature invading the premises. We could have lived without that, and gone on with our routine of washing windows, scrubbing floors, and dipping our fingers into the endless cleaning solutions.

Every spring we opened the Conway house all those years, dusting the parade of books, the Civil War sabers, the nautical paraphernalia, and never once met the Conways. Until that one spring, when there he was—The Admiral, a landlocked widower who needed looking after.

Before, Mother had always said, "I can't figure people who can stand to live in a place like that, a drafty old place with wood floors." But of course, she could never figure out how to live in any of the summer houses that we cleaned, the logs you had to wipe, the bare wood floors needing wax, the small-paned windows that took days to wash and left raw nubs where the ends of your fingers had been. She did not appreciate the interior design of things, for they neither refined nor augmented the way she felt about the place where one should live.

And why should they? When flour sack curtains and hand-braided throw rugs had always been her luxuries.

The Place Where One Should Live. It was like a book she quoted, at the George house, at Duthie's, and the Conway's. "You want to get you a place that's warm, Franki. Not some rat heap that can't keep out the cold. Not like the ones your father always got us. Oh, he gave me a choice all right. After he'd gone all over the country and narrowed it down to just two. Then he gave me a choice, between this rat heap or that. And there was always one of them worse than the other, so it wasn't much of a choice at that."

Mother was always quoting chapter and verse. And when company came to town, all the old relatives from down home, guess where we ended up—driving around the lake and the golf course looking at where the rich people lived. To see the other half's houses. And every time when someone would become particularly attached to a glass chalet or a colonial mansion, Mother would say, "Ceiling sweeper! Knuckle breaker! Rat heap! Don't these people have a lick of sense?"

And that, I thought, was the general estimation of things, how she stood in relation to people at the lake. But then came the retired admiral when I was sixteen, and heaven only knew how old he was.

I mean, it had been ten years since we buried my old man. And he had been a son-of-a-bitch, let me tell you. But that doesn't explain how we felt after the funeral. After the funeral, we all felt warm and good. They made us feel warm and good, about what a wonderful life he had lived. Especially Mother. And especially me. They made me kiss the old man's hard face. And who wouldn't be moved by that? And then they said, the man in the pulpit said, that I would be her comfort, now that her mate had passed on to the grave. Like the old man had always been a comfort.

Anyway, so the man in the pulpit said, I was the one to be her comfort on the rest of the journey of life. And they were true words too, words you could trust. And I was the one she clung to on the couch, in the car, at the graveside. There I am in every picture, right by her side. And I always tried to live up to those words. I was the model daughter. Did everything she said. Hosed off the patio, carried out the dead mice. We had a system. I did outside chores while she stayed in. That's how it was, each of us on opposite sides of the window glass. And I took care of her after the old man died, after my brothers and sisters left home. We worked it out. It was just her and I. And then she wanted to go and bring in the Admiral. How could she think it? How could she do it? To me?—And the old man.

He wasn't much, but I remember when they brought his things down from the woods, where he died reaching up for the tomato soup can he'd just been shooting at. I remember seeing his things being laid out on the table, brought out from the bottom of a flour sack—his knife, his watch, and his wallet with me in the front clip. All that stuff brought out like a treasure from the bottom of the sack made you sorry for something that was gone. It couldn't help but do that. It made us all forget everything he ever did. And you had to honor a memory like that, for all the reasons you'd ever been told, for the things you'd learned in Sunday school.

See even with all his faults, his big plans for raising pigs, she still felt something. He was going to raise these pigs. He had some wild scheme. He was going to get rid of his brood sows because they laid on the little pigs. He was trying to get away with breeding the litter, breeding the young pigs after only one year. And then still sell them for top hog in the fall instead of calling them sows. But he couldn't get away with that kind of stuff, little pigs born without any hair, deformed and dead. That's when she had her miscarriage, my mother. When she was out all hours of the night chasing after his pigs. He was going to make it big in the pig market. Even after that, I know that she still loved him. Even through the bitching.

I listened to her bitch about the way men were for thirty-five years, how they always got their way, how you couldn't use sex against them. Sex was always on the list, somewhere up there with washing windows, between Duthie's logs and making beds. You couldn't use sex against them, when you wanted your way. You just had to go along and keep your mouth shut about things, things like the pigs. That was the way for a woman to be. "Big plans!" she would say. "Big deals on little wheels."

And when I was sixteen, I still thought that applied to all men. All old duffers puttering around the golf greens. But then the Admiral came along and laid his hand across her sweaty palm, and I said, "Can you actually imagine, kissing a rich old fart like that?"

Because I was the child of her old age, the last one, the comfort, the one who was supposed to take care of her, you see, the one who kept her feet warm and slung my leg up over her hip in bed, like Alton had always done whenever she asked. Said it kept her balanced. I was the one. The one with the magic fingers on the backs of her blue-veined legs.

It was just that there was such a big difference in point of view, the Admiral and my mother. You can bet what part of the world he had seen. You know the one about the cross-eyed sailor and the rear admiral. What a cliché that is. A woman in every port, all hands on deck? I mean, what did she know about this guy, really? Other than he had a lot of money. Money he got from who knows where. How in the hell do you get rich in the navy is what I'd like to know. What a pair they would have made after my old man, after baling his hay, and shearing his sheep, and raising his nine kids. What a pair they would have made—the good woman and the rear admiral!

So there they were that summer—the rich old duffer admiral, at a loss with what to do with his hands, and my mother, keeping his house, the house she had always hated to clean. The house that reminded you of a poop deck.

I mean, all this is how I thought about it then. When she began to go around saying, "Of course, these are only their summer homes, their rustic retreats. Their regular places would be much nicer." And they would, too. You couldn't argue with that. You had to go after the man. So I said to her, "Can you imagine kissing that old fart?"

And then one night just last week while I'm digesting pizza, lying half awake to the throb of my own head, I hear her kicking the hell out of a vacuum. And she's been dead three years now, and here she comes back to me in a dream, kicking the hell out of a vacuum. Some Electrolite that you had to drag across the floor. Some worthless piece of junk that was no good for cleaning a house. And she said to me, like I was the old man, standing there in his overalls with the red logging pencil over my heart, she said to me, "What did you buy me a piece of old junk like that for?" Said it to my face, in crisp, clear, apple-biting words. And it made me think about that summer we spent massaging the window glass at the Conway house, those hours we spent gazing out over the cliffs and the lake and nautical miles and velveteen plush carpets, that could have all been ours.

I remembered it all in the middle of a tension headache, about like the one I got now. "What did you buy me a piece of old junk like that for?" she said. They were words like a battle cry. Words about junk. Junk words. And I'm lying there, and I heard again the echoing footsteps down the hall, the hall in the top of the old Woolworth building, heard the thin door rattle when it opened, heard my mother talking when I was six. "I thought this place would be mine," she was saying. "I thought this place would be mine free and clear." And she was pulling my hand up from where I was playing underneath my skirt. "What am I going to do without the money in the bank? How am I going to pay the taxes?" There she was in her flowered cotton dress, like right after the old man died and everyone waiting to be paid. "What in the hell will we eat," she was saying, "while everything is tied up in probate?"

They were her first words really, the first words she'd ever uttered with absolute clarity. They were magic words—words that wanted to shatter glass. And I felt the throb then, like I was feeling it last week, and knew this much, that I was smarter at six than I ever was at sixteen. Hearing those words in the lawyer's office. Words that laid out the unjust inevitability of things. Knew that every time you write "Jesus Saves," somebody would always add "Green Stamps!"

And there we had been all that time. Just one happy family until the old man died. And then he died and I didn't know what we were. Like we didn't exist on paper. Because we didn't own one single thing without the old man.

And what I'm getting at is this. Maybe she should have taken the money and run—The Admiral's. Instead she listened to me. And what did I know? What did any of us know back then, back before the rent was due, back before the world turned nasty. She worked like a dog, cleaning other people's houses until the day she died, for thirty-five years. Alone. That's what my "goodness" did to her. That's how I helped.

"I don't care what anybody says," old lady Hawkins says to me at my high school graduation. "I don't care what anybody says. Your mother did a good job raising you alone by herself like she done. I don't care what anybody says." Said it to me on a whiskey sour and gin fizz. And what a revelation that was. That I had grown up with something missing.

And they were good words too, old lady Hawkins sitting there crying into her glass. Words good enough to live by. Almost as good as the ones they used to paint on Lover's Leap. The ones the ecologists sandblasted all to hell. Gone. All the good words gone.

All but these right here. The ones I've got under the palm of my hand. Saved. Right here. Where they poured plastic over them on top of this bar, so they'd last forever. Universal words. Words you can live by. Are you with me? There! See what it says under there? See, it says, "Old truckers never die—" And you know what that is. That's old duffers, and old sailors, and admirals, and lawyers, and loggers. "Old truckers never die— they just get a new Peterbilt." And honey—you can take that to the bank.